I0622956

Mindblower

By

ALYSIA S. KNIGHT

Heart Dreams
PRESS

Mindblower

By Alysia S. Knight
Published by Heart Dreams Press
Copyright © 2016 Alysia S. Knight
Cover design: by Kelli Ann Morgan @
www.inspirecreativeservices.com

The views expressed within this work are the sole responsibility of the author and do not represent Heart Dreams Press or any of its affiliates.

This is a work of fiction. Names, characters, place and events are product of the author's imagination. Any similarities to actual persons, living or dead, business establishments or events are purely coincidental.

ISBN:-1-942000-19-7
ISBN-13:978-1-942000-19-8

Also available from Alysia S. Knight

 CB80

Past To Die For

Temperature Rising

Kare for Me

Blind Witness

Beauty and the Chief

Trail to Her Heart

His Governess

Her Brand of Trouble

The Ruins – Out of Time

My Spy

Where There's a Will

Aurora Rising

Whistleblower

CB80

To those who serve in all ways.

Chapter One

The roar from the plane's engines and the whipping of air past the open door was deafening, but none of the men on board needed to hear. Zac Masters glanced at the gauges and held up his hand with the appropriate fingers extended for his men to see. Stepping into position, he counted down while watching the dive master. At the go sign, he stepped out into the night-air.

Zac took in the rush of the freefall, and the feel of solitude in the universe. Only a sliver of moon and a few stars not covered by clouds gave light. For a moment, he was alone in the world, then he let reality slide back in and he knew he wasn't. His team was there, at his back. He didn't have to look to know. They moved as one in the air or on the ground. They would be faint shadows just behind him, each in his place, and each covering the others. That was how they worked. It was what made them so good, made them Army Airborne Rangers.

He looked at his readings, on course and near time to deploy chutes. He counted it off, gave a tug. A second later, he felt the jerk as his parachute filled and he started to drift, taking stock of his surroundings. If Intel was right, the opening they were aiming for should be just to his right. He toggled around and made out a darker patch.

The feeling of being watched settled over him, but it didn't come from the ground. He sensed no detection from there. This was a familiar feeling, one he'd grown accustomed to over the last year. It was almost a part of him, like being around his twin, but his connection with Zan was different.

Zac hadn't told anyone about the feeling, not his CO, the psychologist, or even Zan. The first time it happened, it had him questioning his sanity, wondering if he was experiencing ghosts, spirits or something. He still didn't know what the connection was, but there was comfort, concern, someone watching over him. Odd thing was it felt feminine, and in truth, he liked the feeling, liked the touch.

Zac could make out the shadowy shapes of trees and the open mouth of the clearing. Adjusting his course slightly, he moved to drop in. Scanning the area, he prepped for the landing. As his feet touched the ground he darted forward, turned and pulled his chute out of the way for the next man. In less than a minute and a half, they were all on the ground and ready to move.

It was just over a mile to their destination which would normally be less than a seven minute run, but with the thick jungle growth, they had a half hour to reach their mark. They made it in twenty-four minutes, holding their position just a hundred feet from the building that a hundred years earlier had been a church and a mission to help the locals. Now it was held by a man that would be a dictator and his mercenaries, who planned to fund their rise to power with drugs and kidnapping.

Zac pointed two fingers to the right. Alec and Conrad disappeared into the foliage to take their places. With a motion to the left, Steve slunk away, like the other men, not making a sound. Zac waited and watched. Four guards patrolled the outer boundaries. On the far right, one man passed too close to the foliage and disappeared. Zac knew he wouldn't be back. To the left another man disappeared.

Zac held up his hand, then with a slight motion, he crouched low and glided across the ground. He came up behind a guard concentrating on lighting his cigarette. The man never knew he was there before he dropped. Reggie darted passed him to take out the final man by the door. They stowed the men out of sight before taking position on either side of the building's opening.

"All clear," came through his headset from Oscar who had their post position.

Zac heard each man click to affirm they were in place. Alec, Steve and Oscar were the lookouts while he and Reggie went inside to retrieve the kidnapped diplomat and Conrad planted explosives to take out the drug stash.

ೲ

Skye Xavier glanced at the sliver of moon rising over the trees. Clouds crept toward it. It was going to rain tonight. She hurried toward her bungalow wondering what the weather was like a quarter of the world away. She'd know in just a moment.

She looked back at the main building, lights glowed and the sound of the TV blared through the open windows. The faint click of balls on the pool table told her the men not on duty were playing a game to help pass time. This was a boring post, watching a mostly empty compound no one had any interest in. She didn't know why they even bothered with a man at the gate and another patrolling the yard. No one would want to break in here.

It wasn't like when she was a kid and families filled the fourteen houses, plus the men in the barracks. Only seven of the houses were used now, hers, Colonel Sterling, Alvin Botts, the head scientist, Wringer, the other remote viewer and Sergeant Coons, the Colonel's second. Each had their own home. Eight guards shared two more houses and the rest, along with the barracks, sat empty.

Skye wished she could leave, but she had nowhere to go. Besides, what she did was important. Here, she helped make a difference, kept men safe. She looked down at her watch and hurried inside.

It was time. They'd be in the air, almost on target. She

wasn't supposed to know that, know anything at all about the mission, but she'd peeked.

Colonel Sterling wouldn't be happy about that. He'd be out right angry at what she was going to do, but what he didn't know wouldn't hurt her. Skye quickly changed into her pajamas, turned off the lights and stretched out on the bed. With a sigh, she let her mind drift to the coordinates that had been supplied to her two days earlier. Once there, it was easy to hone in on him. She didn't know him, other than the name she'd read off his uniform – Masters, but the feel of him drew her.

Skye was straight over the target when she sensed him. Her heart pounded as she shifted his direction. He drifted. A parachute drop, she let the feel of it run through her, pulling in every sensation. This wasn't her first drop, though she'd never even been in a plane before. She liked the feel.

The ground was coming up fast, then the touch down and she watched him walk out of the landing, taking stock of the other men.

The faces were familiar to her now. Skye recognized most of the men. Knew them, like Masters, because of the names on their uniforms. She'd never met any of them before, and never would. Skye felt an instant of regret, especially for Masters, then pushed the thought away, following them on their trek through the jungle.

They were getting close. The men halted but she stepped out with her mind. Even in the present dilapidated condition, the building was impressive, a simple, mud-brick and stone construction that would've taken a lot of care and devotion to hewn out in the jungle. Trees towered around it. One large tree grew up through the back corner wall, tumbling the piece of the structure like kids building blocks carelessly knocked aside.

A thick canopy of foliage made the building impossible to be seen from the air. To the side and just in front of it, a fire burned in a drum. Not far from it, a man in multi-pocketed, khaki pants and a sweat-stained, olive-drab T-shirt leaned against the wall smoking a cigarette. Skye turned her attention away to look for the other men. She caught only shadowed glimpses of the strike force. If she didn't know they were there, she couldn't have picked out that much.

Masters crossed the ground in a crouched run, with Ramirez right behind him. Masters came up on a man Skye hadn't even realized was there before Masters was on him. Skye looked away only to see Ramirez pass and take out the guy smoking the cigarette. It happened so fast.

Masters and Ramirez took up position on either side of the doorway. Skye let her mind move ahead of them to see what was waiting inside. The only light in the hall was from a smoky lantern sitting on a crate half way to the end, where side hallways split off.

To the hallway on the left were the rooms the mercenaries made their living quarters. Four rooms held a collection of garbage, rough cots or floor mats. Skye decided to check them out, not that she could use the information to help the team but at least she'd know where everyone was. Approximately twenty men slept scattered among the rooms.

She continued her tour much like she had two days earlier when she'd been directed to locate the place and draw up a layout. Other than the fact that it had been daylight on her other foray there, and most of the men were moving about, not much had changed.

The next doorway opened up into what had once been the chapel, now it looked to be used as their gathering and planning room. A couple of long rough wooden tables were strewn with maps and other stuff.

Across from the chapel was the room that held the leader of the group. The room was much nicer than the others. There was no litter and an old cast-iron headboard with a full size bed. The man asleep in the bed looked just as cold as he had during the day as he ordered men about with his hand resting on the holstered gun hanging on his hip. The gun she'd seen earlier lay on the side of the bed by the edge of the pillow.

Skye didn't look any closer. She'd learned on her first adventures in remote viewing to be careful when she entered places so she didn't see things she really didn't want to see. She also learned she wasn't expected to see as much detail as she did. For her, it was like she really was at the location. Even her parents, who were supposed to be the best, could only give rough abstract drawings, though incredibly accurate.

Shifting to the other hall, she went straight to where the man was being held that the rangers were there to rescue. The cell was empty.

Panic hit her. They'd come all this way and he was gone. Was he dead? Skye prayed not. A sick feeling welled up in her, but she forced her mind farther down the hall, hoping he had just been moved to the next room.

It wasn't empty, but it brought even more panic to her. Four men sat around an old wooden table that tilted drunkenly to one side. Though they slouched in their chairs, and it seemed their attention was focused on the game of cards they were playing, they were still fully alert. Scarier still was each had a weapon within arm's reach, two had them lying across their laps; one, leaning against his chair and the other against the wall behind him.

Skye pulled back instinctively, though there was no way they could see her since she wasn't really there, but Masters and Ramirez would be in a minute. The pressing need to hurry had her shifting to the other hall.

She saw the two rangers first. They were half-way down it, moving cautiously to the junction. Skye willed them back, but she had no effect on them, though for a split second she could have sworn Masters paused. They'd continue on until they found their man.

Skye changed her focus back down the hall. She didn't want to go there, but had to look. Had to know. When she'd seen the room before, she'd known what it was for by the manacles pounded in the wall and bloodstains on the floor.

Skye steeled herself and looked. Her heart pounded. The man they were after dangling from the chains. His head hung forward revealing the balding spot on the top. For a second, she thought he was dead until she saw the slight expanding of his chest revealed under the tatters of his once white dress shirt. He was alive, but the team was headed to the wrong place to look for him.

Masters had already turned the corner down the side hall. Ramirez lingered behind, covering his back.

"He's not there." Skye placed herself in front of the lead Ranger. Not that it did any good. A shudder passed through her as he did. She wanted to grab his arm and pull him back, but she had nothing tangibly there to reach him.

He covered the stone floor, each foot placed with precision. Outside the room, he pressed against the wall then leaned forward. He pulled back and made a quick hand motion to Ramirez. His jaw tensed, and he started forward, moving farther down the hall.

"No," Skye yelled. She knew it made sense for him to look. There was only one other room down that way before the building had crumbled under the crushing weight of the jungle trying to take back what had been forged. If the men saw him – she didn't want to think about that.

"No. He's not there!"

Masters froze. His brow crinkling. After a second, slowly, he eased forward. Outside the door he stopped, pressed back against the wall as he'd done earlier before leaning in.

It only took him a split second to take stock of the room then he was moving back down the hall. He made a motion for quiet and another that Skye guessed meant he didn't find the man. They retraced their steps, pausing at the junction before starting across it toward the quarters and the chapel.

"No!" Skye yelled, pushing out with all her will. "The other hall." She tried to force the image into Masters' mind.

He took one more step then stopped, shifting his gazes between both hallways. With an abrupt turn, he headed down the direction she wanted. His movements were as cautious as before but with the assured way he'd moved to the first room. Still, he stopped at the two rooms in the hall to check them out before passing. He didn't seem surprised by what he found. Both were storage rooms just like she'd mapped out.

◌੩ઠਹ◌

Zac studied the hall not sure why he was drawn down this direction. Frustration filled him. He didn't want to believe they had faulty Intel, but Harmon wasn't there. Until that point, everything had been just as it had been laid out.

He tightened his lips as he went over the layout in his mind trying to decide where else they might have him. The other cell had been occupied by a card game. He wondered if it were possible Harmon was restrained down in the main room, waiting for the next video of him to apply pressure for their demands to be met. He hoped that was the case because he sure didn't want other possibilities that came to mind, especially the one that they were too late and he was already dead.

Zac headed toward the chapel then stopped as the utter certainty Harmon wasn't there filled him. He didn't know how but also didn't question as he headed toward what could be termed lightly as the interrogation room but plainly was the torture chamber.

Zac moved quickly, doing it by the book, checking out rooms to make sure they were clear, and they wouldn't be cut off. He found it reassuring when the first two rooms ended up being storage rooms, identical as described. One more door down, he paused and glanced into the room, pulling back before making a more complete survey of the chamber.

The attaché hung, his body limp, held up only by a set of manacles that stretched his arms above his head. He was alive but even the quick glance told Zac he wasn't going to be walking out of there. The man's left leg had obviously been broken.

Things just got a touch more difficult. Zac signaled Reggie then stepped forward to go to work on the lock. A second later, he eased the door open and slipped into the room.

Harmon didn't make a move when Zac pressed his hand over his lips. It took a light shake to get him to stir. Harmon raised his head to reveal split lips, a bruised cheek, and two black eyes. One was swollen shut, but the other was open enough to let Zac see the pain that filled the man. Harmon made an effort to pull back, ripping a groan from him.

Zac made the motion for quiet, tightening his hand over the man's mouth. There was a flinch of pain then Harmon relaxed and gave a slight nod as his brain finally locked in on the fact Zac was there to rescue him.

Zac pulled off his pack, removing the med kit he carried. He didn't have much time, but there were a few things he could do to help the man. First, he did a quick assessment of his injuries. Harmon didn't seem as bad as he'd feared, basically the obvious. The broken leg was a concern but nothing that couldn't be handled.

Having been given medical facts on the man, Zac removed the prepared syringe of pain killers, swabbed his arm, taking only a second to clean the area before giving him the shot. The small inflatable splint came next, stabilizing the leg before he went to work on the manacles. They took the longest and still he was freed in about forty seconds. Zac lowered the man to the ground, then reset his pack, and pulled Harmon up over his shoulder.

Harmon let out a groan but to Zac's satisfaction, tried to muffle it. Zac wished he could just knock him out but couldn't risk it with possible unknown injuries. The pain killer was bad enough but a necessity. Going down on one knee, Zac eased the diplomat up higher on his shoulder then stood. Harmon groaned again, but made no other sound, letting his body drape.

Zac had to give Harmon credit. The man was smart and holding it together, and fortunately, he was in pretty decent shape. He might be a forty-nine year-old paper pusher, but he wasn't carrying more than about ten extra pounds, weighing him in at about a hundred and seventy-five pounds, nothing Zac couldn't easily carry.

Weapon back in his hand, he reached the door, glanced out then joined Reggie at the end of the hall. Reggie made a quick survey of the situation, turned and led the way back toward the entrance.

They had to hurry. Zac estimated almost three minutes had passed. Ahead, Reggie stopped, scanning the area before motioning him forward. Zac just started through the opening when the scuffling of boots on loose rock sounded behind him, followed by a shout.

Zac charged through the doorway, breaking into a hard run. He knew his men would react and have him covered. Still, he made for the foliage. Harmon groaned at the jarring but didn't saying anything, whether because he knew it wouldn't help, or he was too injured to make the protest.

Five feet from the jungle a shot, no louder than the whizzing sound of a bug, passed by from ahead and to the side. A cry sounded from the entrance and shots peppered the area but none came close to him before the pursuer hit the ground.

Oscar had gotten the man but others would be

following. Zac put his life and trust in his men. They each knew what to do. Ahead, Reggie peeled out of the way letting Zac past, coming in behind him to cover his back. More shots rang out from his men laying down cover. A hail of bullets came from the building echoed by the return from his men.

Zac kept moving, knowing internally the time was about up, but he didn't dare slow to look at his watch.

Eight more steps then Conrad's voice came out of the ear piece. "Down."

Just the one word but it was what they were waiting for.

Zac stepped behind a tree trunk and dropped to one knee. An explosion rent the air, shaking the ground. It hardly ended before a larger blast went off. The whole jungle lit up as the inferno reached for the sky.

Reflexes had Zac ducking his head. Behind him, Reggie let out an exclamation as did Harmon. They were up and moving again before the roar ended. Zac set the pace at a ground eating lope, conscious of the injured man over his shoulder, but pressed to get them to safety. Oscar dropped in front of him taking point, making sure the way was clear.

They'd only gone a hundred yards when Alec joined in behind. Conrad and Steve would bring up the rear. Several times, shouts rang out answered by a volley of shots from one of his men keeping the pursuers back.

Every once in a while there were bursts of gunfire from the men chasing them but none ever got close. Zac wanted to shake his head at the stupidity of the guerillas. They were sloppy, used to fear tactics and muscle working for them. Well, maybe not totally sloppy but sure not near what Zac expected from his men.

After only about fifteen minutes, the sounds of pursuit ended.

"Trade off." Reggie's voice came out of the shadows.

Zac was tempted to tell him it wasn't necessary then caught himself. There wasn't a reason not to trade off. It was better to keep himself fresh. "Switch."

They hardly paused in strides moving Harmon over to him. Caution for the man's injures wasn't needed as he knew Reggie would have already taken stock the first moment he saw him. Harmon draped more limply now. Zac hoped it was due to the pain meds kicking in. He wanted to get the man to the pickup location as soon as possible so they could get an IV in him.

Zac brought up a read out. They were only three quarters of a mile from the pickup point and still had twenty-five minutes to make it. He thought about calling in and upping the schedule but decided to hold off until closer, not wanting to give anymore notice to the chopper than necessary if they got slowed down. He shifted into Reggie's spot behind Oscar, looking for any signs of danger. Fifteen more minutes and he checked their location then signaled Alec.

"Get them in. Five minute to rendezvous." A second later he heard Steve relay the information. "Oscar, relieve Reggie." He stepped up to take the lead as Oscar dropped back to take the diplomat. This time Alec helped make the trade, as team medic he took the time to make a quick observation.

"He's holding," he said simply, not wasting time on saying they needed to get him out of there. As one, they resumed the long, smooth stride that wasn't quite a full run but let them move almost soundlessly. Three minutes later, Zac checked the coordinates, in another minute, he brought them down to a walk. Twenty feet farther, the way opened into the clearing they'd dropped into.

The men were silent behind him, a swipe of his hand had Reggie and Steve splitting, each fanning out to check the perimeter, while Conrad stayed back to make sure no one was coming up behind them. Alec had his hand on

Harmon's wrist, taking his pulse. The all clear came through the head set almost the same instant Zac picked up the faint shushing sound of the chopper coming in on whisper mode.

He was moving even before it touched down, taking his position by the open door. Alec and Oscar came next with Harmon. As soon as they had the injured diplomat in, Conrad sprinted forward taking his place on the other side of the door. Steve and Reggie converged on the helo not even slowing on their leap in. Conrad slid in. Zac followed him.

They were in the air almost before his feet cleared the ground. Zac kept watch below until they were out of range then turned to take stock of his men. Alec already had an IV in Harmon with Oscar holding the bag.

"Report," he asked simply.

"All good." The answer came back from all the men. He nodded turning his attention to Alec.

"He's holding. Vitals look good," the man answered without prompting.

The banter of exhilaration erupted from the men but it slipped by Zac as he tilted his head back with a sigh of contentment. One last mission completed to perfection – one last. It was hard to believe it was over. When he got back to the states, he was out. Retired. So hard to believe, but it had been a good run and it was time. The feeling of loss slipped over him followed by another that was harder to explain, like a part of himself slipping away.

The presence that touched his soul was gone.

Chapter Two

He was safe. Skye opened her eyes, staring up at the ceiling in her bedroom. *No,* she corrected in her mind, *they were.* Skye blew out a breath as weariness swamped her body. She was hungry but the thought of going to the kitchen seemed too much effort for right now.

She'd been doing this long enough to know she should've left a snack on her nightstand. But her thoughts had been too locked on him, breaking the rules and watching. Actually, it really wasn't against the rules, no one had ever said anything about doing it.

Skye just knew they wouldn't be pleased, but what were they going to do, fire her? There weren't many who could do what she did. In fact, they were down to just one other viewer, and he didn't come anywhere near to her ability.

Wesley Wringer. Skye wrinkled her nose at the thought of the annoying man, who lapped at Sterling's feet and thought they should 'hook up' because look how powerful their children could be. Skye shuddered at the image of the tall, gaunt man who was a year younger than her and lurked in the shadows when he wasn't locked to his computer.

Skye reached over and found the satchel of lavender and lemon potpourri she kept beside her bed and gave it a light squeeze, releasing the soothing fragrance into the air.

No, Sterling couldn't fire her. He would just find

something else to restrict her from, if he knew, which he never would. Satisfaction filled her, along with the fatigue. *They were safe. He was safe.*

 C3ED

Pounding on her door jarred Skye awake. She groaned rolling over to look at the clock. Eight-thirty. She never slept in this late. Then again it was after four when she finally drifted to sleep.

They were safe. The image of the team lead filled her mind as it had as sleep had over taken her. Masters. She didn't even know his rank, just him. Warmth filled her. *It was silly, but she was half in love with the man she'd never met.*

No, not love. She told herself forcefully. *She was attracted to him, but what woman wouldn't be? He was tall, well-muscled.* Last night, she'd noticed his hair was a little long for his normal military short cut, making it look slightly darker, though, that might have been due to not much light and the camouflage paint covering his face. Skye realized she'd never seen him without the grease paint.

Not that she'd actually ever seen him, or ever would. As far as she knew, he could have been married. But she could dream. Locked away, all she had were her dreams.

Knuckles connecting on her door again made her jump. Pushing her mass of blonde hair back, she stumbled from her bed, past the kitchen through the living room to the door. Not even thinking about standing there in the short-shorts and thin T-shirt she slept in, she pulled open the door and squinted out in the morning sun.

Wesley Wringer's jaw dropped as he stared down at her body like she was wearing a skimpy bathing suit. As if she'd ever consider that.

"Wesley," she said his name to draw his attention up then had to repeat it adding some snap.

"Ah, hi." The man, who if anything, was more inept at

19

dealing with people than she was, stumbled over the greeting. "I didn't see you out and, and was wondering if …" He glanced down at her legs.

"Yes," Skye said to draw his attention up. *Why did he have to be the only one that noticed she had great legs? And it wasn't as if she didn't go around in shorts when the weather was warm.*

He looked up and blushed. "I was …" He cleared his throat. "Wondering if you were all right?"

"Yes, thanks. I just didn't sleep well."

"Oh." He shifted. "None of the men were bothering you last night?"

The question was so absurd she almost laughed. He was the only one that ever bothered her. The guards kept their distance. Mostly, she hoped, because Sterling had warned them off. She didn't think she was that big of a loser. She was – Spook. She knew the nick-name that had been given to her in her teens still floated around. Though she was always treated nicely, with respect, they knew she was different.

"No. I was just thinking about something." She straightened a little.

"I could help you. Or if you tell the Colonel..."

"No, there's no need," Skye added before he could run off and do that. "What was it you needed?"

He shifted side to side and his gaze dropped to her legs before lingering the way up to her face. Skye stepped back, pulling the door closed partially in front of her.

He jerked. "Oh, I was wondering … if you'd like to have breakfast with me. I could fix you something."

The invitation surprised her, but he'd been getting bolder lately. She forced a smile. "I'm sorry. I think I'll stay in this morning and take it easy. I might come out and work in my garden." She knew he hated physical labor and the outdoors, which his pallor affirmed. He'd almost make a vampire look tan.

"You should be nicer to me. I might help you." He burst out like it was a threat, then turned and stomped off her porch.

What did that mean? Help her how? Skye looked around the yard. A foreboding weight dropped on her. She shuddered though the temperature was warm. Closing the door, Skye leaned back against it and tried to push the feeling away. Her talents didn't lean toward pre-cognitive but everything had been feeling different for a long time. A couple years ago, she noticed the first shift when the already trimmed number of people at the installation dropped to the current status.

Skye wondered why they just didn't close this location and move them over to a regular Army base like they'd talked of before. True their project was on the fringes of things but – maybe that was what was happening. They were being closed down.

Another shudder made its way down her body. How would that affect her? She wasn't military. She knew she was classified as a civilian contractor. Which she always thought was kind of hilarious. Though, she wasn't sure what else they could call her – strange person who saw things around the world without ever going anywhere. Self-pity snuck up on her.

For seeing things around the world, she'd never been more than a couple hundred miles from her home, which had always been here. When she was young, before her parents died, they'd gone on a couple short trips.

After, when she was still in her teens, Marta had taken her to the beach once for a week. But Marta had been getting old and not up to traveling much. And by then, Sterling was already pressing her into projects. He always stressed the need of security with her.

Like someone would really want her, someone beside Wesley that is. She pressed down the touch of revulsion and went to find something to eat to replace the calories she'd burned off the night before peeking in on the rescue.

ᏏᎨᏆ

After sixteen hours and a night's sleep on the plane ride home, from a country they couldn't even admit to being in, they landed back on U.S. soil. It was early enough in spring that it wasn't muggy as they stepped off the plane. The smells of nearby woods coming alive with flowers drifted across the tarmac to greet them.

It felt good to be home even if they couldn't enjoy it before they were called in for another round of debriefing. Several more hours passed before they finally broke to clean up.

Zac settled down on the bench, a towel hung around his hips, beads of water trickled down his chest from his hair. He ran a hand back over his head. His hair was getting long. He ought to get it cut. The thought went through his mind before it hit him, it really didn't matter.

For the first time in twenty years, he wouldn't have a dress code. It felt odd, but what would it feel like a week from now, when he was off the base, out in the real world. He'd be back in California by then. Even with Zan there, it was going to be different. Zan was married now.

He gave a slight shake of his head. How long would it take for it to really sink in that he was out of the military? Probably not long. It would be too different. He'd never been one to take much leave, and now–.

"You really doing this, Colonel?" Alec sat down about four feet from him, his elbows dropping to his knees as he hunched over and turned his head to look at him.

"It's done," Zac said feeling a touch of loss along with the thrill.

"I can't believe it. Breaking up the team."

"It's time."

"Yeah," Conrad's lazy drawl drifted up behind him. "He's getting to be an old man."

Zac felt old some days. He'd been an Airborne Ranger

for fourteen years. In command of the team eight of those years. If they had a problem, all the weight of it was on him. He was ancient compared to Conrad who'd only been on the team three years.

"Your last mission." Alec frowned.

"And you guys made me look good. It's the way to go. We got the guy out and all of us in one piece, not even a scratch."

Zac tried to act nonchalant about it, but his stomach muscles clinched. Zan's last op had almost cost him his life. Zac pushed the thought back, he'd had a couple close calls over the years and lost friends. He squelched those memories too, before they could take hold.

"I wouldn't say without a scratch. Oscar always manages to get one of those." One of Alec cheeks tightened to give him a lop-sided grin.

"Yeah, well, I don't count them on him unless it takes more than a dozen stitches. This one wasn't even tape worthy." Zac met the grin, shifting his gaze to the man they were speaking of as he came around a corner.

Oscar shrugged. "I didn't even know I had it until you pointed it out." He shot Alec a glare.

"Hey, it's my job to keep us in one piece and working order." Alec met him with a shrug of his own.

"I think you were just hoping I'd get a shot out of it." When Alec just grinned, Oscar turned his attention to Zac. "You going to see Zan?"

All the team knew his twin. Besides being in the same battalion, Zan's team had been tandem in training and ops with theirs for a long time.

"Yeah. I have a house there that needs building, and we're going into business together. Going to put those degrees Uncle Sam paid for to work. Zan's got a pretty good start going already."

"Can't believe he's married. I never thought he would again." Alec shook his head.

A couple months ago, Zac would've agreed. After Zan's first two disastrous goes in marriage, he didn't think his brother would ever risk another, but, that was until Marley. She was something else. And moreover, she made him happy. Zan deserved someone like her.

A touch of wistfulness hit him, taking him by surprise. He wasn't looking for anyone in his life and there sure weren't many like Marley, beautiful, brilliant, spirited and just plain nice. Women like that didn't come around often, especially for men like them, and to have her drop into Zan's lap.

It hadn't been quite that easy, Zan and Marley both almost hadn't survived their meeting. They were happy now, though, and that's all that counted.

"This one's different. I can tell," Zac said with assurance.

"The twin thing," Oscar said and they all laughed, not that any of them discounted it. They all respected the connection which existed between the two men. No matter where they were around the world, there had always been a link—a knowing.

"He's going to be a father. Marley's expecting." Zac smiled.

"How the great ones fall." Conrad slapped his leg.

"Tell him congrats. Maybe I'll swing by sometimes." Alec reached for a clean T-shirt and pulled it on.

"You're always welcome." Zac followed the motion, donning his own shirt.

"Come on men. It's time for some partying for this old man. We need to send him off right." Alec stood.

A cheer went up and they all starting pulling on clothes.

"You know, I'm still here 'til the end of week." Zac reminded them.

"Why put it off? Isn't that what you are always telling us? We have the Intel, a plan, let's go." Oscar grinned one of his patented grins that made him look like a kid caught sneaking into the girl's locker room.

"That's right, old man. You never know what the week holds." Conrad pulled his head through his T-shirt.

There were some glances exchanged, then they paused when Alec stuck out his hand. "Ever needed."

"Ever needed." Zac placed his hand over Alec's, repeating the words which were their personal motto and made them brothers as much as he and Zan. The others joined in, completing the circle.

ଓଡ଼

Something was going on. The unease was back stronger than ever. All day, tension lingered on her senses like spider feet running up and down her back. Skye shuddered. Why did that thought have to come to her? She hated spiders. They were as eerie as Wesley. He was back slinking around in shadows. And the thing was, she was sure he wanted her to know he was there.

While Wesley was watching her, she got the feeling Colonel Sterling, Coons and Botts were purposely ignoring her. Could it be possible they knew she'd tapped in on the rescue? She didn't know how that would be possible. She hadn't been in the lab with any monitors on her. But, something was up.

The door opened, Skye jumped as Alvin Botts bustled into the building, shutting the door firmly behind him.

He turned and froze at the sight of her. "What are you doing here?" he snapped.

"Just finishing the report from my last session." She watched him. She wanted to say, remember we no longer have a secretary to do that, but didn't. It wasn't that they'd ever been a huge facility but now they really were down to the bare bones.

Botts glanced away not making eye contact with her, nodded, and hurried past to the back of the building. His actions confused her. She wondered, not for the first time, if he was afraid of her, which was truly odd because she'd been his chief lab rat for ten years.

A second later, Skye heard a tap on Colonel Sterling's office door then the little man stepped inside. Skye had just returned to her typing when Coons came out of his office and crossed the hall into his superior's. She tried to concentrate on the report she was filling out, but her attention was on the men behind the door.

"I wonder what's going on?" The words slipped from her as she tried to push the thought away. After sitting with her fingers poised over the keyboard for several seconds without adding a single character to the screen, she gave up and dropped her face to her hands.

She was losing it. What she did was making her paranoid. The possibility she was cracking up hit her hard. Over the years, several of the viewers had burned out. Some became paranoid, others just not able to go on. A few had full break downs.

While Marta was alive, she ran interference for her. At the thought of the old woman who had taken her in after her parents died, Skye's heart filled with sorrow. She missed Marta as much as she did her parents, maybe more.

Marta's death was more recent, and when her parents died, she still had Marta. Now she had no one. No one to love and care for her. No one to keep Sterling from running rough shod over her, as Marta would say. She had nothing but the viewing program. It was all she knew.

Skye couldn't help but wonder again if it wasn't time to get away from it while she did have some sanity left. She actually had quite a bit of money.

There was what she'd saved from her salary, the inheritance that had been held in trust for her from her parents, and an inheritance Marta left her, since she didn't have any family of her own. She hadn't touched any of her saving, living well under what she made was easy because all she had to cover was her basic living expenses; food, clothing, and things for her house. She hadn't needed much to survive.

There were other things she could do besides viewing. If nothing else, she could get a job waiting tables. She could learn how to do that. She also had three degrees. They were all online degrees, but they had to be good for something. Maybe she could open a little boutique and sell her jewelry and crafts she made like she'd always dreamed.

For a moment, she contemplated on letting her mind take a stroll into the office behind the closed door where the men had sequestered themselves. She shook the thought away and forced her attention back to the report.

Her fingers moved over the keys then she stopped as what she'd written fairly shouted at her. *What is going on?*

Skye glanced at the closed door. Her heart pounded. A chill swept over her so strong it felt like the breath froze in her lungs. With all her will, she turned her attention back to the screen, erasing the words, but they lingered in her mind, pulling her gaze back to the door.

Biting her bottom lip, Skye pushed away from the desk, stood, and walked cautiously down the hall. She didn't understand why she was afraid. This was her domain, her world. She'd grown up here, used to play up and down this hall. She'd even played hide-n-seek in this very building with Marta when she was young and both her parents were tied up in the lab or in meetings.

The office at the end of the hall became forbidden to her when she was fourteen and Sterling took over as site commander. Her stomach muscles clenched. Skye stopped in front of the door and glanced back over her shoulder. There was no one else to come in except the guards and Wesley. The guards almost never came in this building since their schedules were posted in the rec room and Wesley would be asleep after pulling an all-nighter in the lab.

Skye drew in a deep breath, leaned forward and

pressed her ear against the wood.

"-pulled," the word said in anger came clearly from Colonel Sterling.

There was a soft murmur that she couldn't make out and guessed it was Botts speaking. Where he could be snide with those whom he deemed his underlings, the man cowered around Colonel Sterling.

"So just won't pay like I thought. I should've guessed. They've been playing with their own program." Colonel Sterling's voice was clear.

"Even with what we've given them, they're a ways out." It was the low, grating voice of Coons.

Skye shivered. It sounded like they'd been giving information from their projects to someone, but that couldn't be. What they did and worked on was classified.

There was another murmur.

"I don't think they can find anyone free thinking enough to." Coons almost sounded cheerful. "It's been bred out of them." There was a second of empty space before Coons continued. "So our golden goose isn't worth an egg."

"Actually," Colonel Sterling's voice reached her again. "We have other offers. One, that when the broker mentioned contacting them, I thought it odd, but they have come back with a surprising offer and can handle our new timeframe. He wants her to take out his competition, leaving him strong enough to take over his country. They want to see some more evidence supporting our claims."

There was a slight mumbling sound, then the Colonel again. "Three or four should be sufficient. Make them ones that the results can easily be verified. Bring me six. I'll make the final selection. Have them ready in an hour."

This time Skye heard Botts's voice, but she didn't wait to hear what he said. Sprinting down the hall, she slipped in the chair and got her fingers on the keyboard just as the door opened. She tried to concentrate on getting words on the page, but hoped he wouldn't look at what she'd written because it likely wouldn't make sense. Luckily, or as was the norm, he didn't pay her any attention.

He was almost through the door when he glanced back. "Finish that report," he said curtly, shutting the door behind him.

Skye was surprised he didn't add a 'now'. She was tempted to close out and leave, but the pounding increased in her chest. Placing a hand over her heart, she drew in a deep breath. *What was happening to her*?

The words were so close to the ones she thought earlier, she glanced back down the hall at the closed door. Coons had not come out. There was no way she was going to go try to listen though. What had they really been talking about? Surely, they hadn't been selling information. Sterling was a Colonel. He seemed to enjoy his post here.

He hadn't been happy at first, she remembered. He thought it was a nut tank. He'd said the exact thing on more than one occasion until he became convinced by the accuracy of what they did.

Again, Skye was tempted to let her mind take a walk and do some snooping. Even if she couldn't hear them, she was fairly efficient at reading lips, not that anyone knew that trick she'd developed. Marta was the only one who'd known she was learning to do it, and she'd urged her to keep it hidden.

At the time Skye wondered why, but since it was Marta, she'd accepted and did it without question. One more thing she was grateful to the woman for.

Skye started to relax to free her mind, when she caught herself. If someone came in there would be questions, ones she couldn't answer. She needed to get back to her place, but first, she had to finish the report.

It took all her force of will to concentrate on getting the words down. Skye knew it wasn't her normal detailed report, but if anyone questioned it, she'd just say Dr. Botts had wanted it finished in a hurry. It was the truth.

She was just finishing the last sentence when the Colonel's door opened. Skye jumped but forced herself not to look back. A few seconds later, she heard a floorboard creek behind her. An eerie weight descended over her.

Swallowing, she looked up, not surprised to see it was Sergeant Coons standing there. Colonel Sterling intimated her, but Coons sometimes gave her the willies. He'd been there for about a year and a half and in that time she'd often felt like he was watching her, it seemed to be more and more lately. She really did need to get away from there.

"What are you doing?" His question was almost the exact as Dr. Botts's, but his voice was more accusatory.

"Dr. Botts wanted me to finish this report." She motioned to the screen, holding her breath when he leaned over her shoulder to read it. A second later, he straightened and nodded.

"Sergeant Coons," she said as he turned away, then couldn't believe she'd actually called his attention. His eyes settled on her again, her throat closed up, and she couldn't get anything out.

"Yes?"

Skye tried to think what it was she wanted to say. *She had to get out of there.* The words came to her mind. "I was wondering if it would be possible; if I could take a vacation?"

His head snapped back as if she had struck him. "A vacation?" he said the word as if it was foreign to him, though he'd taken one just the month before.

"Yes, I haven't taken one in years, and I'm feeling like I'd like to have a break."

"And where were you planning on going?"

She glanced at the calendar on the wall. It was sunset over the Grand Canyon. The amazing vista was lit in vivid colors. "I've been looking at that picture and thought it might be nice to go see it and several other National Parks.

I've never seen any of them. I'd like to."

The dark, straight brows over darker eyes pulled together. "When would you like to leave?"

"I was thinking in the morning. I'm caught up on everything," she added, shifting a little in her seat.

"Not possible. We are expecting an important assignment."

"Can't Wesley handle it?"

"No. This is far too sensitive. And you know he's not near as concise as you are. Men's lives will be on the line."

She knew the added phrase was for effect, and when the image of Masters and the men in his team came to her mind, she knew she couldn't pass on it.

"Tell you what," Coons said, as if reading the decision on her face. "If the assignment doesn't come in a week, you can take some time off, as long as you stay in touch. I'll even get you a cell phone."

The words served to remind her how locked away she was. She was probably the one person in the world that didn't have a cell phone. Still, she wanted to argue, but before she could form an objection he started speaking again. "You know, it really wouldn't be a good idea for you to go alone. Maybe we can arrange someone to be an escort for you."

Did he think she needed a babysitter? "That's not necessary."

"I'll see what I can arrange," he continued as if she hadn't said anything. "A week gives me more than enough time. I will get everything settled." His eyes locked on her. "We can't risk you. You're the whole program." He stared down at her longer than she liked, as if he were saying more, or at least thinking it. His lips twitched, then he turned and walked back to the Colonel's office, knocking on the door before he entered.

This time Skye felt no compulsion to listen. She was sure she knew what was being said – a complete repeat of what they had just covered. Her fingers trembled as she logged off and stood. Pushing the chair back into place, she glanced once more at the closed door at the end of the hall and hurried out.

There were only the two men on duty visible in the yard. Neither paid her any attention. She was Spook, their responsibility to guard. They were friendly but nothing more. She wondered where the others were. This time of the day, someone was usually out washing or working on their cars, or just hanging out.

Skye crossed the yard quickly. Breaking into a run just before reaching her bungalow, she took the three steps in a single bound. Inside she closed the door and collapsed back against it. Her hand went to her chest in a mock effort to hold in her pounding heart as it threatened to leap out. She closed her eyes. A minute later she had enough control back to open them again.

The comfort of the room settled her but still didn't wipe away the last of her unease. This had been her home for as long as she could remember, her refuge from feeling odd and alone in the world. Well, she knew she was odd and accepted it. She knew others could do what she did if they just allowed themselves to believe.

As for being alone, she worked hard to convince herself she wasn't. That was a pathetic lie. She was utterly lonely. She had no friends other than those in the books she curled up with. There were acquaintances in town that she saw on occasion, but no one close. She hadn't even had a boyfriend since she was fifteen. He wasn't even a real, serious boyfriend, but everyone had called them boyfriend and girlfriend, until they realized how different she was.

She was a shadow. She was Spook.

Tears filled her eyes. Skye sank to the floor, drawing her knees up to her chest, her back pressed against the door. It took several minutes of release before she could pull her resolve back around her. Skye pushed the negative name from her mind. She preferred the name she'd come up with for herself. She was Sky-watcher. What she did was important. And now it was time to do some watching.

Pulling herself off the floor she headed to her bedroom by way of the kitchen to grab a snack. What she was going to do wouldn't be going a great distance but to her mind it really didn't matter. It was the length of time she held the view and she wasn't sure how long that would be.

Popping several raspberries followed by a cookie in her mouth, she settled back on her bed and let her mind focus on the building across the yard. She didn't have to worry about the closed door or the walls, she just dropped in.

Coons was still there with Colonel Sterling. They sat across the desk from each other, but they were both relaxed. Sergeant Coons was speaking, but before she could get around to the other side of the room to figure out what he was saying Colonel Sterling looked toward the door.

"Come." The single word was easy to read.

Alvin Botts slid into the room with a stack of files, laid them on the desk, and then looked up like a dog waiting for a pat on his head. Sterling made a slight motion of his hand. The scientist relaxed back. His attention still focused on the Colonel as the silver-haired man placed his hand on the top file and opened it.

Skye saw the confidential stamp, and though she knew he had the clearance, she felt what was happening was wrong. She moved in and only had to read the first couple lines to know what it was. Even before he turned the pages to a series of sketches, Skye knew exactly what she'd see. She should know, she'd drawn them about six months earlier.

Skye could make out two more of the case numbers on other files and recognized them easily. They were also hers.

Sterling pulled the photo page from the back of the file and put it next to the sketch she'd drawn, then slid the open file to the middle-left of the desk. He opened the next folder going right to the sketch and the photo, placing them on top of the file then moved it next to the first.

He followed suit with the others until they were all lined up in the middle of the desk. The sight chilled her because she recognized each. They were all hers, ranging from about two months earlier to about four years.

"What do you think?" Sterling looked up at Coons and motioned his hands toward the files, helping her to figure out what he said.

The sergeant reached out and picked up a sketch and picture, staring from one to the other, before picking up another set. Going through the line until he pushed two back toward Sterling. "Any other should do."

The Colonel nodded and looked to Botts. "Do you …?"

Skye lost the next two words he said, but when Botts looked over the folder and pointed to another, Skye knew he'd been asked for his choice. Sterling tapped a finger to his lips, in contemplation for a moment then motioned for Botts to take the two not chosen away. Botts grabbed them and hurried to the door not needing anything more to be excused.

Coons rose slower. "What do you want me to do?"

Skye was pretty confident that was what he asked.

"Keep an eye on her."

Coons' head raised and lowered before he turned and stalked out. Skye wanted to believe she had got it wrong. She wasn't perfect at reading lips, but she was getting pretty good. She watched Sterling a few more minutes, but he did nothing more than glance at his watch. Finally, she gave up and pulled back, the words echoing in her mind.

Keep an eye on her.

Chapter Three

Skye felt weak. Bile tickled her throat. Dragging in a couple breaths, she managed to keep it down and reached for the snack she'd left on the nightstand. It held no appeal, but she ate it anyway.

What was wrong with her was not from the viewing. It was her suspicions making her sick. She'd bet anything Sterling and Coons were selling the contents of those files. What they had to gain she didn't know.

Skye pulled up the details from the files in her mind. She remembered all her cases. She just couldn't come up with a link between them. They were all old missions, done, and completed successfully. That in fact was the only tie she could think of − they were all perfect examples of missions.

Skye rubbed her hands over her face then buried her fingers back in her hair before pulling them free. She decided that she better do a touch more investigating before she jumped to conclusions. Slightly shaky, she got to her feet.

Halfway down the hall it hit her, she couldn't stay there any longer. She had no confidence in what was happening. Nothing felt right, and it wasn't just the day's events, it had been growing in her for a while.

She looked into the living room, at the furniture she'd picked out and purchased herself a year ago, after falling in love with the pictured room in a magazine. Memorabilia from her parents and Marta were mingled in the bright, cheerfully homey room. Tears threatened her again.

How could she leave her home? The whole house was filled with memories. Her hands trembled. She hated to leave any of it, but, if nothing wrong was happening, she'd be back. And if something was – well, it was time for her to move on. She'd hire someone to come in and pack up her stuff. It would take a moving van for it all anyway, and a place to go.

Living as she did, she didn't spend much, and thanks to Marta, she made a decent salary. Once again it hit her how Marta had been looking out for her. She could afford to have someone pack her up if she decided she couldn't come back.

Now she just had to get out of here.

Another shiver ran through her. They couldn't stop her from leaving. She was worrying herself for nothing. She'd go on vacation. Maybe she'd really go see some of the national parks and along the way, maybe she'd find a place.

Skye shifted direction going into the spare bedroom, getting the suitcases that had belonged to Marta out of the closet. The cases were still in great condition since Marta had got them not long before taking her in and never went anywhere but the one trip.

It didn't take long to throw her clothes into the suitcase, her wardrobe wasn't large. Clothes had never been a big worry to her. She'd always been more of a jeans or capris person. Being on an installation where she was viewed as weird didn't give her much reason to dress up, so she went for comfort, especially when viewing.

Placing the two suitcases by the kitchen door, she looked around and headed to the spare room one more time. Getting a storage tote from the closet, she removed the craft items stored in it and started gathering photos, and her most prized keepsakes, like the lacey shawl Marta had crocheted for her, and several vases that had belonged to her mother.

She filled in the space with the jewelry her mother made as a hobby, which had spurred her own creativity. Skye wished she could take the paintings her father had done, but there was no way to fit them in.

The pictures from the mantle were the last to be packed. She paused to trace the image of her parents. Her father was a tall, slightly thin man from whom she'd gotten her height and green eyes. Her mother was a petite woman with hazel eyes and a hint more red in her sandy blonde hair than Skye had.

They were such a handsome couple. The warmth of their smiles reached out to her. She'd loved them and they'd loved her. They'd always had time for her, no matter what. Even when they were busy, she was their priority.

Marta had been the same way. A woman, who should have been a grandmother to dozens of children never had any kids of her own, so she showered Skye with her bounteous love. Skye brushed back a tear.

Wrapping the last picture, she placed it in the container, sealed the lid and placed it by the suitcases deciding to wait until after dark to sneak them out to her car. It was probably foolishness, but she couldn't help the need for caution she felt.

Having put off what she was trying to not think about, Skye took a deep breath and headed for the lab. She wasn't sure which she was more afraid of. That she'd find she was becoming paranoid and the sinister plot was just in her head, and she was cracking up like many viewers did, or that they really were selling off classified information.

Again the yard seemed too quiet. None of the men were out. Her heart pounded as she entered the code into the keypad. A second went by then another. There was no familiar click of the lock. Had they locked her out? Skye held her breath and pressed the numbers again, a heartbeat passed then a faint but audible click sounded and she ducked inside.

The austereness of the room didn't bother her. Skye hurried down the hall, passed the two viewing rooms, to the vault at the end of the hall. Pressing in another code, this time a green light flashed on immediately allowing access to the room.

A computer sat on a desk to the side, but she by-passed it going right to the file cabinet where all the hard copies were kept. Already having an idea of the dates she was searching for, it only took a minute to realize the first one was missing. Ten minutes more she was certain neither of the other two were there, but the two files Botts had picked up were back.

Skye guessed it shouldn't have surprised her. The files had been on Sterling's desk. She went to the computer, glancing nervously at the door while she waited for it to boot up. The request for the first by date brought up nothing, so she tried subject then location. All failed. Her stomach churned. The file had been deleted.

She tried the other two, coming up with the same results.

Icy fingers wrapped around her like bone-chilling bands threatening to stop her heart. They really were gone.

The threads of hope she'd tried to cling to unraveled. There was no reasoning this away. Colonel Sterling, Coons and Botts were selling information. An unnatural calm settled over her as she shut down the computer and left the building, heading back to her house as she'd done a thousand times before, but this time the way felt unfamiliar.

Out of the corner of her eye, she spied a movement. Her breath caught. A roar pounded in her head. Wesley stepped out of the shadows his gaze locked on her. Skye ignored him. Keeping her pace steady, she reached her house, went up the steps and through the door.

Inside, she froze and looked around. No comfort reached her, only a deep foreboding. She'd leave here and never return. A tear escaped and trickled down her cheek. She swiped at it then stared down at the moisture on her hand.

Funny, she'd never been one to cry much, always too pragmatic. She faced what came her way. She'd done more crying in the last two days then she had in a year. Her thoughts immediately went to a tall Army Ranger.

The last time she'd cried, she thought Masters had been shot. The pain of it flooded back. She'd never forget that awful night. She'd gotten used to peeking in on missions to see how they went. Not necessarily to see Masters, she'd told herself, but that night she'd got there just in time to see the bullet slam into him at an angle that somehow missed his bulletproof vest and still hit him in the chest.

Actually, it had been the other one, his twin. By then she'd figured out there were two of them and they had to be twins to have looked so alike, but they felt different to her. She'd always been able to tell them apart because one drew her with a pull like she'd never felt from anyone else. For a moment, she'd thought it had been hers, even when she figured out it wasn't, she'd still cried for the other.

He'd survived the mission. She knew because she'd stayed with him all the way to the hospital and surgery. It had been a long, painful night and day. It had taxed her past the point of what should have been possible, but she couldn't drop the contact. All the Rangers were special to her, even if they didn't know it.

She'd never picked him, the other Masters, up again on another mission. Skye wondered what that meant. She prayed he had recovered and was okay. Unfortunately, she had no way of asking without letting it be known she was watching their missions.

A combination laugh and hiccup escaped her. More than anything, she wished she could reach out to them now. As many times as she gave out information to help them on rescues, now she needed the rescuing herself. No, she straightened. She didn't need rescuing, she could handle this herself. She'd get up in the morning and leave. It was that simple. There was no need for a rescue. She was a free person.

With resolve, Skye settled down to fix a dinner of her favorite oriental-styled chicken salad. While eating, it made her think of taking some food with her, which led to gathering a lot of other things. Pulling out the backpack she used for hiking, she loaded it with her first aid kit, flashlight with new batteries, pocketknife, change of clothes, and jacket, food and her purifying water bottle, because you just never knew.

After cleaning up, she settled down with a book by one of her favorite authors, but for once, it wouldn't hold her interest against the oppressive weight settling on her. She'd have to find someone to report what was happening. It was treason or something like that. Whatever, she couldn't let it go on.

Too uneasy to sit, she made several rounds through the house rechecking the locks on doors and windows. From the spare bedroom window, she could just glimpse the main gate. As usual, it was locked up for the night. She was safe. Funny, she didn't feel that way.

Skye picked up the book again. A half hour finally passed but she couldn't remember what she'd read. Another trip through the house proved the windows were locked. The whole yard was quiet. The lights were even out in the barracks. She glanced at the clock. Twenty-five after twelve. Looking out the windows showed once more no sign of anyone out or movements in the deep shadows left by the bright floodlights.

In the kitchen, Skye picked up the larger of the two suitcases and went out the back door, making sure the screen didn't bang. Keeping close to the house to stay in the shadows, she made her way around the side to where her car was parked.

Skye flinched when she opened the trunk and the light came on. She hadn't thought about that. Quickly, she hoisted the bag inside and lowered the lid, leaving it open just a crack. She went back for the tote then the smaller suitcase. With the car locked, she dashed back to the house, fell against the door and flipped the dead-bolt she'd installed herself. Tonight she was more thankful than ever for the touch of security.

Nothing was going to happen, she reassured herself as she changed into shorts and an old, comfortable T-shirt. Because of training for her viewing Skye was usually very good at relaxing. Stretching out, she endeavored to clear her mind. Thoughts and fears assailed her. Skye drew in a deep breath and reached for comfort.

The image of a man filled her mind. Tall, broad shoulders, muscled arms, close cropped hair – a military buzz was how she thought of it. His light-colored eyes blazed amid splotches of black, brown and green covering his face. The paint didn't detract from his strong chin, high cheek bones and sharp nose. Without the grease paint, it would be a ruggedly handsome face.

Even as she tried to hold the image it shifted, not fading, but changing. Gone was the camouflage paint. There was just a hint of softening around his lips. He lay flat. His eyes closed.

Panic hit Skye for a minute, almost pulling her free as he was so still she was afraid he was dead. A cry escaped her. Pain ripped at her heart, then his chest rose and lowered with a deep breath. He stirred slightly.

Skye stepped forward, watching intently to confirm the action. There was no missing the movement under the taunt T-shirt covering his chest. He was breathing. She looked around the room taking in the details. It was a small utilitarian bedroom. Her gaze went back to him. He was sleeping.

She wondered where he was. Was he in the United States or on a military base somewhere around the world? He was a Ranger which meant he could be anywhere in the world.

Cautiously, she walked to the bed. She knew she wouldn't wake him. She really wasn't there, just her mind was, and she was intruding on his privacy. It was wrong, but she couldn't stop herself. His presence drew her in.

Skye couldn't help but wonder about him as she had on so many other occasions. Was he married? She hoped not. That would really make her pathetic. Spying on and fantasizing about a married man.

She glanced at the hand resting on his stomach. There was no ring. That didn't mean anything. She knew some men didn't wear them in combat areas for safety sake. Still, he was alone in bed, which she was extremely grateful for.

He wore a military issue T-shirt. A blanket lay bunched around his waist covering the lower part of his body. He had one arm curled above his head.

Skye reached the side of the bed.

He brought the arm down in a motion that seemed to reach for her. For an instant, she was tempted to take his hand, then pulled back. Not that she could actually touch him. Still, she longed to touch him like she never had wanted anything in her life.

What was she doing torturing herself with what could never be? Skye started to turn away only to be pulled back. Her heart pounded. She wanted to go to him. He pulled at her, offering a security she wished was real.

"Please, help me." Skye couldn't keep back the words as they slipped out. Everything she was facing burst over her and she had to fight to hold in the tears that threatened her again. *"Rescue me."* She didn't know why she added the plea before she turned and fled back to her own body.

She opened her eyes, forcing the air in and out of her lungs. Slowly, her breathing returned to normal. She pushed the fears that had snuck up on her away and concentrated on the man who seemed to hold solace for her. She didn't let her mind reach out again. Instead, she wrapped the image in her heart and let the comfort of him fill her.

⚬⚬⚬

The woman slipped into Zac's dream. He knew she was there, but just couldn't quite make her out. Still, he felt like he was breathing her in. She came closer. He tried to reach out for her but couldn't make contact. Frustration filled him. Why couldn't he touch her? He knew she was for him. Knew she was the woman he'd been waiting for all his life.

He tried to bring her clearly into his mind. He wanted to see her. Was that asking too much, to see her, to know her other than the whispers in his dreams and phantom brushes across his mind?

Light, long willowy movements fluttered on the fringes of reality. Eyes like soft green jade glowed with mysterious depths waiting for him to step into them. He could just about make her out then she pulled back.

"No. Don't go."

She turned back to him and a shiver of fear burst from her. *"Please, help me!"* Her plea went straight to his heart. *"Rescue me."* Panic hit him. He reached for her again, but she was gone.

Zac jerked awake and sat up. Dropping his feet to the floor, he stood and turned in a circle searching for her. Light from the street lamps outside cut through the blinds he'd left partially open. The room was empty, but she'd been there. He would've staked his life on it.

He knew the feel of her though he'd never experienced her presence outside an op before. What did that mean?

"Help me. Rescue me." The words came with such need they staggered him. He sat back on the bed. She needed him. He had to find her. The only problem was – he

didn't know who or where she was, or if she was even real.

Zac dropped his face into his hands and rubbed his fingers up, over his head to the back of his neck. What was he thinking? No one had been there. It had been a dream. His imagination.

"It's a good thing you're getting out. You're losing it," he said aloud. Maybe he should postpone leaving for a few days and talk with the base psychologist before he left.

"And tell him what, a beautiful, green-eyed woman called to me from my dreams." Zac laughed at himself. "That said, seventy percent of the guys on the post would need to be in counseling."

He shook it off and stretched back on the bed, tucking his hands behind his head. He could come up with the Doc's answer himself. It was getting out and not feeling needed anymore. He was a rescuer, a man of action, and now he was facing a big change. Zac pushed away the fact that thoughts of her had been going on for well over a year.

He willed himself back to sleep. Ten minutes went by then twenty. It became apparent sleep wasn't going to come.

He glanced at the clock. Five-thirty. He'd be getting up in a half-hour anyway. He sat back up, dropping his feet to the floor. Not a bad idea to hit the gym for an hour before he got ready to go. He'd be driving a long way today.

Sweat poured off him by the time Zac finished his work out, but it helped to clear his mind. He headed for the showers feeling right with the world. He was ready for the day, ready to head home, see his brother and meet his new sister-in-law.

The thought of Zan married brought a smile to his face, and they were expecting a baby. Man that was fast. Hey, but at their age, it was probably a good idea to start on the ankle-biters while they were young enough to keep up with them. He wouldn't mind helping raise a couple. Though, he figured he'd raised enough recruits to fill his quota of fatherhood responsibilities.

He turned on the water and stepped under the spray. He was going to miss his military life. He'd never say it aloud, but it was there. He'd liked the life he led. There had been some young knuckleheads that turned into some fine soldiers – fine young men. No, there were no regrets.

He turned his face up to the spray, letting the water sluice over him.

"Rescue me." The words came back to him.

"I'm afraid I'm leaving that for the younger guys," he said aloud and pushed the image from his mind, reaching for the shampoo.

He took breakfast at the officer's lounge then went to find his commander to sign his final release papers. A half hour later, he stood on the steps a free man, relieved of duty, with all the good-byes said.

Zac blew out a breath. It felt odd. Had Zan felt this way? He'd been coming off a medical release when he'd gotten out. Weird.

Zac headed for the temporary housing where he'd stayed the last two nights after vacating his apartment. It only took a moment to change out of his dress uniform and grab his duffle bag to head for his truck.

The gleaming white beauty sat waiting for him. Zac tossed his duffle in the back seat, hung up the clothing bag with his dress uniform. He removed his personal weapon from his rucksack and stowed it in the lockbox he'd installed under the seat.

His other guns were being shipped along with his other stuff. He didn't have a great deal of belongings to worry about. As a bachelor, he had a big screen TV, a loaded computer and a comfortable bed that held his six-four frame. He didn't mind sleeping in the dirt or in a tree when it was called for but when he was at home, he wanted his comfort.

Everything was already headed for Zan's house, where

it would stay until he got his house built at least enough that he could move in. It shouldn't take long. He didn't need much, just running water, some electricity and his bed. He could even make do with a sleeping bag for a couple weeks. He smiled. He had no desire to intrude on the honeymooners too long.

"Hey, Colonel." Automatically, he turned to see Conrad hurrying toward him. "Not anymore," he said to the younger man. "I'm a civilian now."

Conrad met his smile. He would always hold his rank to him and all the other men that knew him. "Glad I caught you."

"What's up?" Zac asked.

"Wanted to ask a favor. You can say no if it's a problem."

"What is it?"

"I was wondering if you could drop this off at my parents in Scottsboro. It's for my Mom's birthday tomorrow. I didn't expect it to get here in time, since I didn't order it before we got sent out. But it just arrived, and you sounded like you were going to do a little wandering. I hope it's not too far out of your way."

"No problem." Zac reached out, took the box Conrad was holding before the young man could pull back the request. He placed it on the passenger seat and turned back to Conrad. He'd been to Conrad's parent's house before. His mother was great. A warm, welcoming woman who went to a lot of work to feed her son's comrades off on a fishing trip.

"Thanks. Can you give her my love?" He shifted a little, color heightening his cheeks.

Zac understood. There were few men in the military that didn't have a soft spot for their mothers. He remembered his with fondness. He reached to take the held out hand and was pulled into a one armed man hug.

"Thanks, sir," Conrad said.

"Be safe," Zac countered back.

"Will do." Conrad released him and stepped back watching while Zac climbed into the truck and pulled away.

Zac glanced at the mirror. There was an unreality, knowing he wouldn't be back. He blew out a breath.

Five minutes later, he drove out of the base's main gate and pulled over, taking one last good look back. "Time to make a new life," he said to himself. Taking a picture, he sent it to Zan without attaching a message.

The phone rang before he could even drop it into his cup holder.

"On your way?" Zan asked without greeting.

"My parting view," Zac said.

"How's it feel?"

"You know."

"Yeah," Zan answered. "I should have come."

Zac laughed. "I'm okay big brother."

Their looks and personalities were so alike, it was almost strange. They'd never had the good twin bad twin thing, the competition, or even older sibling younger sibling differences. They enjoyed the same things, faced things the same way, and had identical work ethics. They were friends as well as brothers.

"I know. We'll be looking forward to seeing you. Keep me posted on your travel."

"I will, but I'm in no big hurry. May do a little meandering. Gonna start by dropping off something for one of the guys."

"Sounds like a plan. See you when you get here. Marley's dying to meet you."

"Sure it's not just morning sickness?" He couldn't help but tease.

"She's not doing too bad with that. Though I did find out she can't handle fish right now."

"Got it. I won't suggest we go fishing when I get home." Zac smiled.

47

"Not for a couple months, unless its catch and release and we get the smell off us before we get home."

Zac laughed.

"Heard there was a storm headed your way?"

"It's off the coast. I'll be a long ways away even if it makes it inland."

"Just take care."

"Yes, dad." Zac grinned. "See ya."

He disconnected, dropped his phone in the cup holder, shifted into drive and headed west. It was a long way to California. He flipped on the radio. Country music filled the cab. Maybe since he'd be in Scottsboro he ought to swing up by Nashville. It wasn't far out of his way. He'd take the scenic ways and enjoy the sights, do a little hiking. After all, he had all the time in the world.

Chapter Four

Skye came awake to sunlight streaming in the room. She stretched, playing over the image of the man from her dreams. Masters. For a moment, she let her mind run its fantasy of him there to hold her and keep her safe.

Safe!

She sprang up, attention going to the clock. Seven twenty-two. She'd overslept. Not that she had a timeframe to leave, but she'd planned to be gone by now, at least before everyone but the morning guard was up moving around.

Skye jumped from the bed and dashed to the shower. Ten minutes later she was out and dressed. With her damp hair hanging down around her shoulders drying, she poured the last of the juice in a glass, and drank it while fixing a bowl of cereal. She ate as she dumped the rest of the milk down the drain and checked the fridge for anything else that would go bad. Tossing the lettuce into the garbage, she stopped, realizing how odd her actions were. She was supposed to be fleeing, not cleaning the house.

She was pathetic, but it was still her house. Grabbing the garbage along with her purse and backpack, she locked the door and headed for her car. The morning was beautiful with only a few high clouds. But, if she remembered right, there was a storm brewing off the coast. So she'd head northwest to get away from it. That worked with her plans anyway.

She turned the key in the ignition. Nothing happened. Not even a click from the starter. Trying again she got the same result. Skye got out and lifted the hood. Thanks to Sam, one of the older gentlemen who was there during her teens and enjoyed teaching her about cars, it took her less than a minute to figure out what was wrong.

The wire to the starter had been cut. She shuddered. There was no doubt it was intentional. Not only had it been cut but a good portion of it was missing. There wasn't near enough for her to have a chance of splicing it to get to somewhere so she could replace it.

Had someone seen her put her suitcases in the car? She was being watched, and they were trying to keep her there. Skye grabbed her purse and backpack and headed back into the house, going right to the phone. She wasn't surprised at all when there was no dial tone.

Though it felt like steal bands were contracting around her chest, she drew in a deep breath and went over her options. The lab had no phone but there was one in the office building and one in the barracks' main room. The choice was clear. She really didn't want to chance the office, so it was the barracks. Deciding it would be wise to keep her ID and money with her, she put her purse in the backpack, slipped into the straps, and headed for the barracks.

The screen door was ajar, and as was common, the other door wide open. No one was in the main room as she entered. She waited, listening. Voices came from the kitchen area. Skye eased over to the phone, lifting it carefully. Placing the phone to her ear, she glanced toward the kitchen. Her heart pounded so loud it took a second to realize, like her phone, no dial tone sounded in her ear. It too was dead.

She knew all the men had cellphones. She just didn't know who she could trust to ask to borrow one from. Skye moved back toward the door then stopped, getting caught up in what she heard.

"Should've left with the others." The grumbling carried across the room.

"What's the hurry? I'm going to miss this post," The voice came from the other room. It sounded like Jackson, a young, red-headed private from Minnesota.

"You're kidding? Not me. Out here in the middle of nowhere." One of the guys, Ray, she thought, answered.

"Not that far," Jackson corrected him.

"Twenty minutes just to reach Podunk town." The words confirmed the identity. Ray was from New York City and didn't like the rural area at all. "Can't even get cell phone service half the time, and it's an hour to get to any town of decent size."

"I thought you enjoyed Janeen's company."

There was no answer that Skye heard.

"Come on," Jackson said, "You can set out and relax. No one is shooting at us. We have a clean place to stay when you do your dishes. Normal food."

"Normal!" Ray's comment cut in and was ignored.

"As light a duty as you can get."

"Guarding something no one's interested in. And, the only woman on the place is off limits."

"You've got to admit, she's great to look at," Jackson said.

"Yeah, but you can't touch. Even if she wasn't off limits, you know she's strange. This whole facility is about her and the freak."

Even though Skye had heard the words before they still cut.

"She's not weird. Skye's nice. I've never seen you complain about the cookies and things she brings around."

"Yeah, nice, and I didn't say I wasn't interested. There's not a man alive that wouldn't be interested."

"Just because she's so out of your league." Jackson laughed.

"Right." There was a loud snort. "More like, not worth the effort. It would be writing your ticket to the worst hellhole on earth if any of us looked at her with the least degree of interest. Coons made that very clear my first day here." Ray grouched, sounding like he'd really been put off by it.

"We all got the lecture by the colonel or Coons. Wonder where she'll be going?"

"Who knows, they'll probably lock her away some place. Really wonder what it is about her that's so all important."

"Ours is not to question," Jackson said sagely.

Skye pulled back, making her way for the door. She halted on the steps, trying to take in what she'd heard.

They were being shut down. She looked around the empty yard. The men were being reassigned. How many were already gone. It sounded like Ray and Jackson were the only two left. That's why it was so quiet.

Why hadn't Coons told her? Why had he insisted she had to stay? He had to have known. What was the plan for her? The chill she'd been feeling for the last couple days spiked. She rubbed her arms. She needed to get out of there.

Did she dare ask either of the men for help? They were her friends, kind of. Jackson was at least, and a couple others, but were they under orders to keep her there? She couldn't risk having them tell. That left getting to the phone in the main building, the building that housed Colonel Sterling and Sergeant Coons.

Skye jumped off the porch, ducked around the end of the barracks, and ran for the main building, slowing as she reached the steps. In two days, she'd gone from a normal, open life to slinking around like Wesley.

She paused with her hand on the door and eased it open. No sound reached her. Skye slipped inside, her gaze going to the hall. The doors to both Sterling's and Coons' offices were closed. She wished she could believe they weren't there but didn't dare. They both kept tight schedules.

Sterling would've been up running the perimeter of the installation at six-fifteen. Even at his age, he never missed a morning. Then he'd go in and lift weights for a half-hour before being at his desk at eight o'clock sharp. It wasn't unusual for Coons to have a similar routine, with one exception, he would be in the office at a quarter to eight to be ahead of the Colonel.

Nothing else to do but try, Skye dashed across the room to the desk, reaching for the phone just as she heard a door open down the hall. She dropped to the floor behind the desk, praying Coons wouldn't be coming that way. Fortunately, his attention was focused on Sterling's office.

He entered not bothering to close the door behind him. "You wanted me?"

"Just got the news." Sterling's deep voice carried. "Those new files helped to spark more interest. So joined back in and they got into a bidding war."

"He wanted her after all."

"I don't think he really believed there was another buyer. He thought he could get her for a steal." Smugness rang in the Colonel's voice.

"What'd he pay?" There was no missing the glee from Coons.

"Not enough. Vibora got her. Nine million dollars."

Coons let out a whistle. "Our little golden goose came through after all. When's pick up?"

"Details are still being worked out, but looks like Monday night they'll be set to smuggle her out of the states."

"The sooner, the better."

A phone rang. Skye jumped and looked at the device in her hand.

"Coons," the sergeant answered before Skye realized it

was his cell phone and not the phone she held. "I'll be right there." He disconnected. "The last two are ready to go."

"Good. Get them off the installation and lock it down," Sterling ordered.

Skye pulled deeper back in the corner, praying more than ever that he wouldn't see her, but there was no need for concern. Coons went out the door, his gaze not varying from straight ahead.

Skye had no doubt of the 'her' they were talking about. There was only one 'her' on the installation.

They were selling her!

'So' was not a word, it was a name. And who was Vibora? She shuddered. Nine million dollars. For her. And where were they going to smuggle her out to? The only thing she understood was the why. Her viewing.

No way. She wasn't going to help a foreign country. Or a drug lord. What she had heard before played over in her mind, 'take over their operation and country'. Plans were to use her to find stashes of what she guessed was drugs or encampments.

She had to get out of there now. Glancing at the phone in her hand, she wasn't at all surprised when she raised it to her ear and found it dead like all the others. They'd cut the communications to the installation and were sending the men away, leaving her locked inside. Well, that wasn't going to stop her.

Staying low, she crab-walked across to the door. Cracking it open, she peered outside making sure no one was there before she slipped out. From the end of the building, she saw Jackson's old, beat-up truck followed by Ray's flashy, little, red sports car drive through the gate which started to close the instant they were clear.

Instinct had Skye wanting to run after them, but she knew she'd never make it. Instead, she turned and ran the other way, bypassing the barracks and her house. She had her backpack and it had all her necessities.

Skye skidded around the next house and stopped. Flattening herself against the building, she glanced back. Coons was striding away from the closed gate, head high, arrogance poured off him. He always had that look, but until now it never registered just how much it bothered or frightened her.

She watched until he went back into the building. Well, if they thought they had her trapped, they had another think coming. She'd been a child here. She knew a couple escape routes, if she could still make it. Doubt hit her. Skye pushed the thought away, turned, and screamed.

"Wesley." Skye sagged as relief hit her. Her hands came up to cover her heart. "I didn't see you."

"Not surprising the way you're sneaking around."

"We –" Skye started to warn him, then it hit her. They hadn't said anything about Wesley. They only referred to her, and all the files had been hers. Were they not taking him? Was he in on it? She definitely didn't trust him enough not to be careful.

"I'm not sneaking. I just had to think. Did you know we're being shut down?"

There was a minute tightening around his eyes that if she wouldn't have been watching him so closely, she would've missed. "What makes you think we're being shut down?"

"I saw them packing, and they just left."

"So what?" He shrugged, but it wasn't very convincing. "So they're leaving. Nothing big about that."

"All of them?" She straightened.

"I doubt it was all. And maybe they got transfers."

"All of them?" Again, she pressed.

His shoulders raised and lowered once more. "It's no big deal. Nothing for you to worry about."

"How can you say that? It is a big deal. We are being shut down, and they didn't even tell me."

"If you needed to know Colonel Sterling would have

said something to you. Let's go talk to him, and we can get this straightened out right now." He reached for her arm.

Skye pulled back.

He looked shocked at her action but kept coming, forcing her against the side of the house. Feeling crowded, Skye struck out, but he caught her wrist jerking her around to face him.

"Let me go." She struggled against his grip.

A snort sounded from deep in his throat. "I don't think so. I told you that you should've been nicer to me. Now, I think we better go see the colonel."

"No, Wesley. You don't want to do this. Something's going on. It's not good."

"That all depends on your perspective." He pulled her forward.

"No!" Skye kicked out. He tried to shift to avoid it. She followed the motion driving her free hand into his stomach. His knees buckled, and he dropped to the ground. She turned to run, but he grabbed the bottom strap of her backpack. Skye thought for a second of releasing the straps and pulling free, but not wanting to lose the pack, she settled on the more direct action.

She kicked out again, catching him on the side of his head. Wesley lost his hold and fell back with a groan. His eyes closed. Compassion yelled at her to make sure he was all right, but self-preservation won out. She ran, taking the path that headed away from the buildings and into the trees.

There were two options and both were on the back fence which was about a mile away. Her first choice was about a quarter mile along the fence where trees hung over on both sides. It meant playing like Tarzan, but was preferable to wiggling through a tunnel filled with water and possibly water moccasins.

Funny, as a kid she never worried about them. It had been just one more great adventure. Well, now it wasn't an adventure. It was life or death, or at least freedom, and she didn't want to contemplate the alternative.

The main trail wove through the forest shielding her. She was almost where she would need to cut through the trees to reach the fence when she heard the sound of a vehicle coming up behind her. Skye veered off the trail into the growth and ducked low.

There was only one reason for anyone to be out there. They were looking for her. She didn't wait to see who it was. She just kept running through the thick growth letting memory and instinct guide her.

Skye glanced over her shoulder afraid any second she'd see the vehicle. The sound grew closer. She dropped to the ground behind a thicket of wild rose bushes. Her heart pounded in her chest as much from fear as the run. She waited, afraid any moment the sound would stop and they'd find her.

It kept on, coming closer, moving slowly.

Skye held her breath though it wouldn't make a difference for those searching for her. Seconds ticked by in her head, then the sound of the motor faded. Silence took over the woods. She continued to wait for the noise to return but only the sounds of birds and bugs did.

Skye waited another minute and started through the thick brush. After four hundred feet, the woods abruptly ended. Twenty feet from the edge rose a high, barbed-wire topped fence that was supposed to bring security. Instead it loomed dauntingly.

Glancing in both directions, Skye turned left. Staying close to the foliage, she ran, watching for the trees she wanted. After what she guessed was almost an eighth of a mile, despair crept in with the fear.

Had one or both of the trees been cut down? She didn't know. It was possible, she hadn't paid much attention to them in years. Another possibility hit her. Had she turned the wrong way and the trees were behind her? She didn't think so.

Skye started to swing around to look back and caught a glimpse of a large tree extending over a flowering dogwood. She raced forward then sighed in relief at the sight of the two huge trees stretching toward each other over the fence like forbidden lovers.

It had been years since she'd climbed a tree, but it didn't slow her. Skye made the jump catching hold of the lowest limb and placed her feet against the tree, walking them up until she could swing a leg over the branch and pull herself up. She puffed in air as she sat straddling the limb.

From there the branches were closer together, offering hand and foot holds. About twenty feet above the ground, she walked out on the branch that extended over the fence, using a limb above her head to steady herself.

She was almost directly above the fence when the branch started to sag and creak under her weight. Breath caught again in her lungs as she edged closer to the branch reaching out from the other side.

Skye was concentrating so hard it took a minute before the sound of a motor penetrated her mind. She looked down to see the olive drab military vehicle driving along the edge of the fence less than two hundred feet away. Sterling was at the wheel with Wesley, the weasel, beside him. So far neither seemed to have seen her, but all it would take was for one of them to glance up.

The thought was hardly across her mind when Wesley shouted and pointed. "There!"

Sterling pressed down on the gas as he looked her way.

Skye didn't wait to watch them further. Pushing caution aside, she hurried hand over hand and her feet sliding forward. There was a popping sound from the branch and it dipped slightly but she didn't stop as the other branch was now just a foot away. One more step and she reached out and caught another overhead branch. This one was a stretch to reach, but she used it to add momentum to her forward motion.

"Halt!"

She ignored Sterling's order and pressed for more speed as the branch grew firmer under her feet. She was on the other side of the fence now.

"After her!" Sterling barked.

"But," Wesley's protest reached her.

Even from her precarious perch, she could hear the quiver in his voice and smiled to herself.

"Don't let her get away."

The gangly man scrambling out of the jeep spurring her on. Reaching the trunk, Skye glanced back in time to see Wesley make the jump and catch the branch. He slipped off and fell to his feet. Sterling had his cell phone at his ear.

Skye started down, almost slipping off a branch in her haste. She reached the bottom branch as Wesley managed to pull himself into the other tree. Her branch was a good eight feet up, as the lower branches had been cut away.

It was an intimidating drop but the sight of Wesley reaching the branch she'd walked out on had her dropping to her stomach, letting her legs hang down. She lowered herself until she was stretched fully out then let go. She landed on her feet but the jarring impact had her falling back to end up on her seat.

"No!" Sterling yelled at her.

Skye met his gaze and pulled back at the fury in his eyes.

"Where do you think you're going?" He took a step toward the fence. Before he could do more, he froze at the same loud crack that had her flinching and looking up.

There was a cry then another pop and Wesley and the branch crashed to the ground. Wesley cried out again then groaned curling into a ball on the ground.

Skye felt a grin start to rise in her but it faded as Sterling took another step. "You'll never escape." Promise dripped from the words.

Skye pulled herself up and ran. Wesley's groans faded along with Sterling's threat.

ৎৡৼ৹

Zac hummed with the music and reached for another homemade cookie from the large bag Conrad's mother had given him. The woman had a big heart and could sure cook. He bit into it, savoring the taste. Well worth the side-trip. As was the scenery along the small scenic road he'd opted to take.

He discounted the strong pull that had drawn him off the main road. It was beautiful country; rural, hilly with foliage so thick you'd be lost in it just feet from the road. He hadn't seen anyone for miles. Usually when he was in a place with this kind of solitude, someone would be shooting at him before he was out of it. No more of that.

He took another bite of the cookie enjoying the wave of contentment for another mile. Unease hit so hard and so fast he barely kept from jerking the wheel and sending the truck into a skid. All his combat training had him looking around but he didn't see anything.

The feeling of shadows closing in behind him had him glancing in the mirror then back at the road. A chill ran down his spine. His chest tightened. There was nothing there.

The problem was the reason he was on the road. There was really only one way to explain it. He hadn't been just drawn – he'd been compelled.

He popped the last bite of the cookie in his mouth and reached for the comfort he'd had a moment earlier. It didn't come. Zac took in a deep breath, filling his lungs then let the air out slowly. Hunching his shoulders, he tried to relax the muscles one by one in an exercise he'd learned over a decade earlier. Peering out the windshield, he took in the beauty.

The tension remained.

Maybe he should head straight home and forget the wandering. It might be he was just missing his own section of woods that were so different from these. When he hit the next highway, he'd head right to the interstate and California. The calm he thought the new plan would bring didn't come.

Danger crackled in the air.

He leaned forward looking up at the sky expecting to see clouds boiling up. It was still clear blue. The weather changes weren't supposed to be brewing in until tomorrow. Another reason to head straight west, though this far inland the tropical storm off the coast should lose a lot of its kick.

Zac glanced over at the cookies and sighed. Slowing the truck, he reached his arm over the seat, grabbed the strap of his backpack and lifted it onto the front seat. He fumbled with the zipper while keeping his attention fixed on the road. He placed the bag of cookies inside.

"You just never know," he said aloud, justifying his action to himself. He blew out a breath, drawing the line at the impulse to stop and remove his gun from the lockbox under his seat. He was not in danger. Another mile passed and there was still no one out there.

"Maybe I should have talked to a counselor before I left. I'm jumping at shadows, or at least looking for them," he said aloud, making the decision to retrieve his gun.

He slowed taking the next curve then hit the brakes as a figure burst out onto the road in front of him. His hands locked down on the wheel as he jerked it hard over, sending the truck into a skid to keep from hitting her. The truck jolted and rocked, coming to a complete stop on the side of the road facing the opposite direction.

Adrenaline burst with him from the truck. "Are you−?"

"Please, help me!" The words sparked right out of his dream though she said them aloud.

She ran toward him, struggling for breath as if she'd been running a long time. With each step she took, he felt a little breathless himself as he took in the sight of her. Then, before he could do anything to stop it, her foot caught a crack in the pavement. The cry that escaped her ended abruptly as she hit the ground. Zac reached her in a heartbeat, forcing himself to take stock before turning her over. Her body quaked in its labored pants to pull in air.

Zac reached for her then stopped, his hand hovering just over her shoulder, not quite sure if he dared touch her. "Are you all right?"

She drew in two more deep breaths then pushed to her side. Green eyes the color of jade stared up at him. "Please!" They pleaded without her saying a word. Then as if really seeing him, her eyes widened in shock. She jerked slightly. "Masters."

Zac could swear she breathed out his name, but it was so soft he knew it couldn't be.

"It's …" She didn't get more out as the need for air hit her so strong, she gulped in breath.

"Easy," he said as she flinched, pulled back then gasped this time with pain. "I won't hurt you."

She shook her head, and he wasn't sure if she was disagreeing with him or dispelling the notion. He hoped the latter.

Her eyes darted over her shoulder down the road. "I need to get out of here. Hurry." She started to climb to her feet then almost fell again before he caught her.

"Easy," he repeated. "Let's get you in the truck and check you out first. Just hold on." He slid his arms under her and the backpack she wore. He stood, lifting her, not giving her time to protest, not that she did. A gasp escaped her as her arms wrapped around his neck. Her eyes met his, and he couldn't move. Shock so powerful filled the green depths, she appeared to be looking at a ghost instead of him.

Zac felt an echoing reaction surge within him. He'd swear he knew her though he was certain they'd never met.

It was her eyes. The dream came back on him. 'Help me.' The words jerked him into action. Crossing to the truck, he placed her gently onto the seat he'd just vacated.

The urge to raise his hand and touch her cheek was so compelling it was all he could do not to follow through with the action, then she reached up and cupped his cheek. Her thumb a breath away from caressing his lips.

"You're real." Awe filled her whisper then she jerked back. "We have to go." A panicked cry took over and her gaze darted to the road again.

Zac heard an engine and turned to the sound.

"No, hurry." She was already tugging on his arm as she slid across the seat to make room for him.

Instinct had him following her onto the seat. "It's all ri −" Zac cut off at the sight of the jeep with two men in it, coming around the curve. To his shock, an arm extended out from the driver's side. There was no mistaking the object pointed their direction even before the shot cracked. Zac dove over the woman, flattening her to the seat.

Chapter Five

"Down!" Zac yelled.

He heard the shot but there was no sound of a bullet hitting the window or the cab.

He fumbled for the lockbox, cursing himself for not listening to his instinct a moment earlier. Another shot stopped his action. Glancing over the hood there was no way he could get his gun before the pair in the jeep reached them. He stretched out for the key still hanging in the ignition as another shot rang out.

Zac felt a minute shift in the truck.

Tires!

He got it. Whoever was shooting at them wasn't trying to hit them, just stop them from getting away. They were shooting out the tires. He didn't want to guess how many were flat but, depending how good of a shot the man was, two at least, maybe three. He wasn't waiting around to find out.

He reached over the woman for the door-handle. "Go!" He forced the door open and her out in one motion. Luckily, she understood what he was saying and scrambled out without resistance, staying low when she dropped to the ground. Following her, Zac grabbed his backpack strap slipping it over his shoulder as he landed. Once more, he wished he could get to the gun locker but a glance over the hood revealed the men getting out of the jeep. He wanted to get a look at them but didn't have the time to spare.

"Go!" He locked hold of her arm and dragged her off the road into the undergrowth. Staying low, he cut a trail not giving her any choice but to follow. Not that she seemed inclined to object. She stayed with him, running crouched, full out without qualm.

Behind them he heard a shout as the men reached the truck and found it empty. "After them. Get her." The order cut clearly in a manner fitting a drill sergeant.

Twigs and branches snapped as the men pushed through, showing these guys weren't into hunting or had spent little time trying to evade detection while moving rapidly. They crashed through the growth. Elephants moved quieter Zac thought. His companion definitely was more cautious. He continued on, weaving their way deeper into the trees, not slowing even when the noise of pursuit grew fainter then subsided entirely.

He continued to drag the woman on, her wrist shackled in his fingers. It didn't matter that he didn't know her name or who she was, he had to save her. The memory of green eyes flashed in his mind. 'Help me.' He would!

A small outcry accompanied a jerking on his arm. Zac spun in time to barely catch her before she impacted with the ground. One look at her had him lowering her down and crouching beside her while she fought for air. Her eyes were shut tight in her labors. Zac was tempted to hush her, but the only sounds escaping her were the tiny gasps for air.

Senses open on full alert, Zac scanned for any telltale signs of pursuit. He couldn't pick up any. They'd lost them, but training had him opting for caution and not speaking. So he studied the woman on the ground. A pinkish-orange T-shirt and well-worn jeans hugged her trim body that was shaped to draw a man's notice. Her hair was a long, light-brown almost blonde. Trapped in a holder behind her neck, it flowed down her back almost to her waist.

She was lightly tanned, not dark like the women who favored tanning beds or spent all their free time at the pool, but the tan like those who like to be doing things outside and used sunscreen. Her nose was smaller, giving her a fairy-like appearance. Her eyelids fluttered open revealing her large jade eyes. As he studied her, he changed his mind from fairy to a very serious wood nymph.

"Are you okay?" Lame question, he'd just run her near to death with people shooting at her.

Still, she nodded and wet her lips, drawing his attention to them, not like he hadn't already noticed them. They were on the full side, and a soft pink that beckoned to him. They parted slightly as if giving him the invitation.

"Yes." The answer he was hoping for slipped out. He about accepted it with his mouth when he realized it was the answer to the question he'd asked.

She sniffed. Her eyelids dropped closed but not before a tear escaped.

He caught the drop before it could trickle down her cheek.

Her lids sprung open, but her eyes showed no fear as she met his gaze. "Thank you." Her voice was smooth with just the barest hint of a southern drawl.

Zac nodded. Then realizing his fingers still lingered on her face, he drew his hand back. "Can you go on? I'd like to get farther away, though I think we've lost them."

"Yes." She gave a slight nod, her teeth catching her lip again, but determination filled her eyes.

"We'll be moving slower. More carefully to make it harder to track in case they're still after us," he told her in way of encouragement then extended his hand down to help her up. Awareness burned in him as her hand slipped into his. He drew in a deep breath, bringing her into him. He knew her. Again, the certainty washed over him. She was there on the edges of his mind.

Her eyes darted over his face. She felt it too – the connection. He pulled her up with the thought of bringing her into his arms but she released him and stepped back before he could give in to the foolish urge.

They needed caution and to get somewhere safe.

Zac turned, settling into a slower pace, cutting a trail while trying to take stock of their location. He knew which way they were headed and where the road was in reference to their location. The smartest bet would be to parallel the road then swing back to the truck, coming in from the opposite direction.

The question was – would his truck be drivable if it was even still there. He hoped it would be. Besides his gun being in it, his cell phone was still sitting in the cup holder, not that he'd been getting any reception out here. He needed a sat-phone.

They went what he figured was another quarter mile when they came up on a rocky ledge over a ten foot drop off. A small stream cut down through the bottom of it. Zac decided to hold up there for now. When he stopped and turned, she almost ran into him. He caught her arms to hold her up.

"Sorry," she steadied herself. "I was looking around. It's actually very pretty here."

"No problem. Listen, I want you to wait here. I'm going to go back and find out if we're being followed." He saw the flicker of panic before she could tamp it down. "It's all right, I won't be gone long. I won't leave you here."

"I know." Again there was the certainty in her. One of utter faith, though she didn't even know him.

"You know, I don't even know your name."

"I'm Skye. Skye Xavier."

The oddness of her name struck him, but he decided he liked it. "Zac Masters." He held out his hand. She studied it for a moment before taking it. He didn't have to wait for the awareness to hit him. He would know her touch anywhere. "I won't be long. Trust me."

"Further and faster."

He nodded in acknowledgement. He needed to let go of her hand but couldn't make himself open his fingers. He forced himself to back away, their arms extended out between them before they finally released. "Be careful around the rocks. There are a lot of snakes around here."

She nodded.

Zac took one last look, drinking her in before he turned and headed back the way they came in at easy run. He was about back to where she'd fallen and they had stopped when her words hit him. 'Further and faster'. She hadn't said farther. The Ranger creed said 'move further and faster'. Did that mean she knew he was a Ranger? There was no way.

He slowed to a stop, going back over everything in his mind. His uniform was bagged, not visible. There was nothing there that he could think of to tell, not even a bumper sticker, like some of the guys had, on his truck because he didn't like them. He ran his hand over his head. His hair was short but nothing too unusual. They were hours from the base. How had she known? Did she? Had she called him Masters earlier? What was going on here?

One thing was sure – someone was after her. So he'd better get his mind on business. It didn't take him long to track back to where the man had given up and turned around. In a muddy spot, Zac could tell one man wore a smooth-soled shoe with a heel, the other man wore a gym shoe, the canvas type, and scuffed his feet.

Zac was tempted to follow them back to the road but decided it would be better not to leave Skye that long. He would stick with his original plan and curve back around to the truck. First, he had some questions. Zac took time to covers their tracks, though he didn't think there was much need. Whoever had been after Skye had given up, or at least changed tactics. He let his mind worry over the problem as he ran.

Why were they after her? She'd been their clear intent.

'Get her', proved it. Why? What could she be involved in? The obvious answer that came to his mind was drugs, but as the image of her filled him, he had trouble believing that. She didn't look the type, if there was a type. It was more likely he didn't want to believe it of her.

Zac hadn't reached any conclusion by the time he neared the area he'd left her. He needed answers but as soon as he saw her sitting on a rock with light coming through the trees on her, his heart did another jolt, stopping him in his tracks. He was in trouble. He was half in love with a woman he didn't even know.

C33ΩO

Skye tried to calm her insides. It all had to be a dream. None of it could be real. The installation closing. Sterling and Coons selling her off. Masters here. He was the final straw kicking it out of the realm of possibility. He was at his military base wherever it was. Probably halfway around the world doing other missions, saving other people. He couldn't be there – saving her.

No matter how much she wanted it to be true, it couldn't be. Awareness tickled across her nerves. Skye turned and there he was twenty feet away, tall, strong, powerful. He was better looking than she'd thought. His face a little more chiseled. A hard chin with a slight cleft that shouted he didn't back down.

She'd grown up around military personal, but she knew of no one that would measure up to him. Sterling commanded, but Masters – Zac, his name whispered over her heart, lead with confidence that others naturally followed.

His eyes reached her over the distance separating them. Light blue, stormy at the moment. Something was bothering him. Unease trickled in. Had he run into Sterling? Were they close? What happened?

Skye stood as he came toward her, letting her back pack drop to the ground.

"Skye freeze!"

She obeyed. Just her eyes moved, going to the cinnamon colored blur as it shot out toward her leg. Skye felt a jolt and watched in shock as the snake pulled back then slid into the undergrowth. Still she couldn't move and her heart hammered in her chest.

"Skye?" The hand on her arm drew her back to reality. "Sit down. Let me see."

"I —"

"Sit down." Zac pushed her down, not waiting for her to comply, dropping to his knee in front of her. "That was a copperhead. Even if that was a dry bite, it needs attention." He was reaching to pull up her pant leg. His hand ran up her leg over her calf, in the most intimate touch she'd ever experienced from a man. "Where?"

"I don't think it bit me." Skye managed to get out. His hand held her enthralled.

"You're certain?" His gaze came up to meet hers.

"Yes. There's no pain. I-I think it struck my backpack instead." The instant of fear evaporated into complete awareness. Zac was so close she could smell the spicy maleness of him. It wasn't at all strong or obtrusive to her, in fact, she found it very pleasant.

She followed his attention as it dropped to the canvas bag by her foot. Skye felt a loss when he removed his palm from her leg to lift the bag.

"You're sure?" He looked up at her.

Skye could only nod. The reality of what happened robbed her of her ability to speak. Tremors broke out, swamping her body in violent quakes. The next thing Skye knew, she was locked against warm, hard muscle.

"Shh." The hiss in her ear was soothing as was the hand that rested on the back of her head, pressing her deeper under his chin. "Shh, I've got you."

"This can't be happening." Skye clung to him, praying he was real. The arms around her tightened. Skye was glad because she was afraid they were the only thing keeping her together. It had been so long since she'd been held or comforted. She never wanted to move again. Unfortunately, after a few minutes, the hold eased and Zac shifted back.

"I really need to check again to be sure." His gaze ran over her face. He raised his hand to brush his knuckles over her cheek. A forced smile crested the corners of his lips, then his eyes rested on her lips and grew intense.

Her breath caught for a whole different reason. For a moment, Skye thought he was actually going to kiss her. She wanted it more than anything, then his focus dropped back to her leg and he lowered his hand, cupping her calf once more in his palm. Lifting the limb, he ran his fingers over the skin inspecting it thoroughly. "I don't see any marks, though you do have a bruise here."

"I did that climbing the tree."

His head jerked up to study her again.

"Long story." She winced at the thought of it.

"One I think you better tell me. Now." He added more forcefully on the end.

Skye winced. She knew this was coming, just not quite sure what to say so it didn't sound crazy to him. For once in her life, she really didn't want to be crazy, weird, strange, or spooky. Why did he have to be the one to find her? Her fantasy. Couldn't she have something, even if it was only in her mind; something to dream about?"

When she didn't say anything he came up with a question. "How did you know my name?"

Her brow furrowed, and she tilted her head slightly to look at him. "You told me."

"But you called me Masters before that." He let that soak in only a second. "How do you know I was a Ranger?"

"Was? But … were?" She broke off when his eyes tightened. Skye put her hands to her temples and rubbed. Had she been viewing into the past? She didn't think so. "I don't understand."

"Well, if you won't tell me that. Let's start with, who's after you? And don't deny that. After getting shot at and running through the forest, I think you owe me that much truth."

Skye shook her head. "They were after me."

"Why?"

Taking a deep breath in and letting it out slowly, she told the truth. "They want to sell me." The reality of it made her start to tremble again.

The muscles around his eyes tightened. "Sell you?" The words didn't come out easy.

She nodded. "To the highest bidder." Skye knew she'd surprised him. It was on his face as was the speculation of why, though she guessed his hypotheses didn't come close to the truth.

"Something tells me we're not talking prostitution or human trafficking?"

She could feel he wanted her to deny it, but Skye shook her head.

"But you're certain they were selling you?"

She shifted to raise and lower her head. "I heard them finalizing the deal after a bidding war."

His brow arched again.

She continued, going for broke. "Nine million dollars."

That shocked him. "What?"

The urge to cry exploded in her, but she fought it down wrapping her arms around herself as Zac studied her. She was sure he thought she was crazy now. One look at her, and there was no way someone would think she was worth a tenth of that. She was ready for a snort or at least laughter, but none came.

"I think you better back up and tell me more." He kept his voice even.

Skye sighed, knowing she was going to slip from weird into the being crazy category. She didn't know which was better, but he deserved the truth. "I work on a," she winced, "special government, military project."

His brow arched but he didn't say anything.

"One that people think doesn't exist, or at least no longer exists. Which, I guess now doesn't, since I found out this morning we've been shut down."

The eyebrow remained arched.

Skye wet her lips. "I found out those over the project are selling me to a foreign country."

"So you're saying espionage?"

"Yes, I guess that's what you'd call it. Though, I hadn't thought of it that way. I found out first they've been selling or giving away information from different projects I worked on. Most of that information is classified."

Skye waited for a reaction, but none came. He just stared at her like a statue with burning ice blue eyes. She took a deep breath and blew it out. "I found this out last night and was going to leave when the gates opened this morning, but my car wouldn't start. Someone had messed with the starter. None of the phones worked. All the guards had left, and they locked the gates after them. I snuck into the main building and overheard them talking, about the bidding being complete, and they were handing me over on Monday. So I ran."

"How'd you get out if the gate was locked?"

"There's a place at the back of the installation where the trees grow up and over the fence on both sides."

"So you climbed the tree?"

She nodded. "I went out on a branch until I could reach the one on the other side. Only they discovered I was leaving and came after me."

"Who's they?"

Skye winced. "The installation commander and his second; also the doctor, research not medical, and one of the other guys is helping them. I don't know how much he really knows. He's more of a stooge, I think."

"What is it you do?"

Skye bit her lip and looked away, not wanting to answer.

"Is it classified?"

She sighed and looked back. "Yes and no. What I do isn't really classified just my projects are."

His eyes bore into her. "So why would someone buy you?" He came back to that.

"Because of what I can do. The information I can give." It was the truth Skye thought. She just made it sound a little different, hopefully normal.

"Do you know who's paying for you?"

He was persistent. She wasn't surprised. "At first, I think they were hoping for an Asian government, but it sounded like someone out bid them."

"Someone?"

"They called him, 'vi bora'."

His eyes left her to look away into the rocks and bushes were the snake had disappeared. "Vibora." He finally repeated the word, much closer to how Sterling had said it.

"Yes. You know who they were talking about?" She leaned forward, but he was already shaking his head.

He swiveled back to look at her. "Vibora means viper in Spanish. Snake."

A chill ran over her as she, too, glanced to where the copperhead had disappeared. The trembling started again in her body. His hand settled on hers pulling her attention back to him.

He squeezed lightly. "Skye, what do you do?" he asked her straight out.

Skye tried to steady herself. If he was going to think she was insane or a freak, it was better now than later. She cleared her throat. "I'm a remote viewer."

She cringed, waiting for either of the normal two reactions she'd gotten most her life, either the pull back, or the most common – the question, what is that and then the pull back. Neither came.

He just stared at her. After a minute, he finally spoke. "I thought that project ended almost ten years ago."

Shock settled over her at his calm acceptance. "It was wound down then. They closed the main location and cut back most of ours but somehow we remained functioning on a limited basis."

"Ten years ago you'd have been a child." He still didn't seem overly freaked, but he was like a man working through a puzzle.

"I had just turned fifteen."

"Fifteen. How?"

Skye gave up. It was all going to have to come out so she decided just to tell him. "It's a long story. I was raised on the installation. Both my parents were viewers and researchers. I showed signs very early of having strong inclinations. Then came the publicity about the government doing physic research and the cutting of the project." She shifted to the side, glancing at him.

"We were getting ready to leave when my parents were killed in an auto accident. They'd gone to California for job interviews. I was staying with the secretary here. She was kind of my adopted grandmother. My parents didn't have any other family. After they died, she applied and got custody of me. Then somehow, though the installation got cut back heavily, it remained open. Gradually, because I was there, I began viewing."

It hadn't been that gradual. More like whenever Sterling, the new commanding officer at the time, could coerce Marta into her doing it. Skye understood even then she was the most accurate viewer they had.

"Who's over the installation?"

His change in questioning surprised her. "Colonel Sterling."

"Colonel?"

75

She nodded.

"You said he is behind selling the information?" Zac released her hand and stood, taking the few steps to look over the ledge down at the stream.

"Yes, and Sergeant Coons, his second in command."

"Do you know who was in the jeep shooting at us?"

Skye wrapped her arms around her knees. "That was Sterling. It's his personal jeep. I think it was Wesley Wringer in the passenger seat. He's the only other viewer there. He caught me right after I overheard everything and tried to stop me from leaving."

Zac turned back to her. "Tried?"

"I hit him in the stomach and ran."

He smiled, approval lit his face.

"I should have hit him harder. I'm sure he told the Colonel. That's how they found me going over the fence. Wesley tried to follow me but fell out of the tree." Skye found herself smiling, feeling quite satisfied. "I was hoping to make it to the road and get some help to get away before they caught me. I didn't think I would get anyone shot at."

He came back and knelt in front of her. He placed his hand under her chin and tipped her face up to meet him. "I'll help. Do you understand that? I'll do everything I can to keep you safe. First of all we need to get back to my truck. Okay?"

Skye nodded, hardly able to comprehend he seemed to believe her, and he didn't look at her like she was a freak. At least, he was going to help her.

A large hand appeared in front of her face. She followed it up. He didn't flinch or look away but met her gaze. Skye would swear he was asking her if she believed him. She almost smiled at the oddity of the thought. She placed her hand in his, and it was engulfed by long, work-roughened fingers. With just a light tug, she rose to stand in front of him. He towered over her. Skye wasn't sure she'd realized how tall he was as she tilted her head up to meet his gaze.

"I will help you, Skye." There was no mistaking the intensity in his words as they filled her. Zac Masters would save her, but she felt like something more was being said. She just didn't have the experience around men to know what it was. Still, never in her life had she felt so right. For a second time that day, her whole world shifted and realigned.

Chapter Six

Zac fought the urge to pull her all the way into his arms. Just a touch more force and she'd be there. His body remembered the feel of her. Slim, trembling, utterly feminine. He wanted to hold her again, to comfort her, but she needed something else from him. She needed Lt. Colonel Zac Masters, Airborne Ranger and all the skills he brought.

"Let's go." He released her hand. "Tell me if you need to slow down or rest." He turned to weave his way back through the woods, leaving her to follow.

They hadn't gone far when she spoke up. "Can I ask you a question?"

"Sure."

He wondered when she'd get around to asking about him. After all, she was putting her life in the hands of someone she didn't know.

"How do you know what a remote viewer is? Most people have never heard of them and don't believe they really exist. You don't seem to have a problem with the idea." Trepidation swam in her voice so strong he was surprised she'd had the nerve to ask.

"I have a twin brother. We both joined the Army and have had similar careers. After we'd been in for about four years, we were approached about having some testing. The officer thought we might be good candidates for a special project because we were twins and were known for being close."

"You believe you have a link with your twin?"

"Zan."

"Zan. You have a bond with him, don't you?"

"I won't deny it. We also had a commanding officer at the time that warned us it could be bad for our military careers. It's an intriguing notion though, so we did do some investigation in into it, and like our commanding officer said it would have drastically alter our service. At that point, they were on track on how we wanted them, so we weren't interested." Zac shrugged. "Can you do what they said?"

She was silent a moment.

He was about to clarify his question when she answered.

"Yes."

He glanced back over his shoulder. When she saw him, she looked away. He stopped and turned to face her so quickly, she ran into him. "You can really see into other places?"

Pain etched in her features. He didn't understand why, but she nodded, raising and lowering her head slowly then pulled back.

"That is amazing. There are no restraints on distance?"

This time she shook her head.

She seemed embarrassed. When she wouldn't meet his eyes, he started walking again. "What's it like?"

There was a slight pause. "It's like dropping into a location. I usually don't know what to expect. Most of time I'm just given coordinates. I concentrate on them then I'm there. I try to walk through and observe all I can. When I'm done, I come back, make a sketch, and write up a report describing all I observed in detail."

"How clearly do you see things?"

"Pretty clear." There was a pause. "As in, it's like I'm really there."

"That must be scary." He glanced back.

"Sometimes." She took a deep breath. "I never know what I'll find. A lot of time it's just a building or a bunch of buildings with people walking around. If it's at night, people might be asleep." She hurried past that point. "A few times I've dropped into some bad things."

Zac could tell she was nervous talking about it but had to ask. "Like what?"

"Tortures." She sounded choked. "People getting shot." She fell silent.

Zac didn't know what to say to that. He'd seen a lot of the bad stuff, and evidently so had she.

They continued to walk for a while, then it hit him. She wasn't surprised when he said he had a twin. In fact, she'd said something earlier that almost suggested she knew. She also knew his name. "How did you know my name?" he asked the question flat out.

"I've seen you on missions before." There was definite timidity in her answer.

"You've watched?"

"I wasn't ever told not to. At first, there were a couple of missions that I really wanted to know what was going on," she said defensively. "Overtime, I started to recognize some of the men, and I got concerned. I wanted to know they made it back safe."

She fell silent again but his mind kept going. She cared about the men and needed to know they were okay. She–

"You knew I had a twin." He looked over his shoulder in time to see her nod.

"I figured out there were two of you. It took a while but there was something different in you."

"When he was shot, you knew?" It wasn't a true question but she answered.

"I was watching."

"So you watch everyone?"

"Not always but when possible. It was my information … and I was worried."

"So you saw when my brother was shot." He could hardly believe it.

"Yes." The word squeaked out from her.

"It wasn't your fault. From what I understand the information was accurate."

"It was. It was just bad luck the man was out smoking a cigarette at the time and looked up." Pain and fear came through her voice. "I tried to warn your brother and some of other guys. But couldn't because physically – I wasn't really there."

"So people can't tell when you're there?" He turned and looked down at her, trying to understand fully.

"No."

He studied her face in the fractured light coming in through the tree. Zac could swear a slight blush colored her cheeks. "Are you certain of that?" He wanted to tell her he'd known she was there, but for some reason couldn't force himself to divulge that fact yet. There was so much more he needed to learn about her.

"I'm not really there." She glanced away.

Unable to resist, he placed his hand under her chin and turned her head back and up so she had to look at him or close her eyes. "Part of you is there." He followed the impulse running through him and dipped his head brushing his lips over hers.

Her eyes were wide when he pulled back. Her mouth opened in a sweet little O that he wanted to take command of. Instead, he turned and started through the growth once more. A second passed before he heard her follow.

ᘓᎂᘔ

Skye wasn't sure what had just happened. Her lips tingled and her heart pounded, and it wasn't from exertion. Zac Masters had kissed her. It hadn't been a long, drawn out, passionate kiss, but from her very limited experience, it had been the most incredible kiss in her life. She could still feel him there, like he had sealed himself to her. She touched her tongue to her lips and swore she could taste him and a touch of chocolate chip cookies. The thought almost made her laugh.

She was losing it. After everything that happened she really was slipping out of reality. But, he really had kissed her, and he hadn't freaked out about what she did. There were no odd looks, derogatory remarks or names, just acceptance.

Skye stared at the back of the man in front of her, and her heart continued to pound. She wasn't sure what to think. She didn't have any experience to pull from. Zac Masters was way out of her league. Not that she actually had a league. Still, the man was handsome with a capital 'H'. Not gorgeous. He was too powerfully built for that; hard and chiseled.

Zac's back view was as good as his front, due not entirely to the backpack he carried, his T-shirt pulled tight over muscled shoulders and thick biceps. Skye followed the pack down to a trim waist, then looked away, trying not to contemplate his tush, but it really looked nice. Even the slightly baggy pants with their copious pockets couldn't mask his taut frame.

It hit her, he was still wearing his regular army pants and boots. What was he doing here? She tried to ignore the question, and just be grateful he was, but couldn't get around it. It was too much of a coincidence. "Zac, how did you end up here?"

"This frantic woman came running out in front of my truck. It was either run her down or stop."

"Zac." A smile came to her as she realized he was teasing her. She enjoyed the feeling it brought for a second then turned her attention back to her question. "You were in the jungle earlier this week." If she hadn't been so close behind him and watching she would have missed the flexing of the muscles in his arms.

They covered about twenty feet before he spoke. "So

you were watching?"

"Yes." Skye saw no reason to deny it.

"How long did you observe?"

"Until you were on the chopper headed back."

ᏨᎦᎬᎠ

"And, when did you start?" Zac had to know. There was a long pause this time. He glanced back at her. "Skye?"

"I came in when you were parachuting in."

Zac wondered if she meant she came in with him, but decided not to pursue it. "All right. Well, that was my last mission. As of this morning, I am officially out. I retired and am now on my way home to California."

He could hardly believe the reality of it. "So, I guess you could say coincidence, but maybe fate is a better word, though I don't think I've ever put much stock in it before. I'm more practical and think we direct our own lives. It is something though that I was on the right road when you needed me." He didn't want to say he'd been compelled there, but it was there at the back of his mind. He had been drawn to the spot.

"I don't know. There is so much out there we don't understand. I didn't realize until I was already viewing that most people thought what I could do was impossible. Strange."

The last word was tacked on so quietly Zac wondered if it was her thought that reached him and not that she'd actually said it. "You said you were raised around it?"

"Yes. We were at a large military base when I was real young. I think I was about seven when we came here. I started second grade in the town about fifteen miles from here. There were quite a few kids on the installation back then."

"Any of the other kids became remote viewers?"

"No. Not that I know of. There were only five or six viewers. Most everyone else with kids moved out by the time I was fifteen. My parents were the last to go."

"So you were the only young person there from then on?"

"A lot of the guards stationed there weren't much older," she said so quickly it screamed of her loneliness.

As young as she was, especially as pretty, they wouldn't have come near her. It would have been a fast track to a court-martial. His heart pulled for her. He'd grown up with his brother and family around, and went to a school with a lot of friends. They'd been on the football team, played soccer, baseball and volleyball. They'd always been doing things with someone, if not, they had each other.

"What do you like to do?" His question came out on its own.

"I like to read. I do crafts. Make jewelry and other stuff. I always wanted to learn to blow glass or do ceramics but there's no one around to learn from. I love to ride horses. One of the guys here used to have a couple horses that were actually housed at the installation, but he retired a year ago and moved back to Colorado."

Again there was a wistfulness in her voice. She'd never make a poker player. If Skye felt something, it tended to come out.

"Why don't you get your own horse?"

"I've been thinking about it. I even went and looked at a couple, but they weren't … right. I'd also like to get a dog, I think."

"What kind?" That caught his interest. He thought about getting a dog when he got home. His life hadn't been conducive for having one before, but he liked dogs. He and Zan had a golden retriever while they were growing up.

"I don't know for sure. Something big that I can go on walks and runs with, maybe even play catch."

The image of her out playing with a retriever came to his mind in sharp detail.

"Do you like dogs?"

"Yeah, I'm thinking of getting a retriever when I get back home."

"You're headed to California, now then?"

"Yeah, my brother and I inherited some property from our grandfather. Zan's house is pretty much complete. I just have the plans for mine. We're starting a business together."

"What kind of business?"

"Electronics. We both have engineering degrees and have always liked to tinker building things. Being in the military has giving us a few ideas on things that would be useful or need to be improved upon." He shrugged. "We'll have to see how things go. We already have interest in one of our inventions."

"Can I ask what it is?"

"We–" Zac broke off, picking up some subtle changes ahead. His hand went up in a clenched fist motion for halt before he thought about the fact that Skye wouldn't know what it meant. To his surprise, she froze and crouched down.

"What is it?" she asked in a whisper that barely carried to his ears.

He turned to face her straight on to reassure her. "We're getting close to the road. I want you to stay here while I go check it out."

Her lips parted with an intake of air then she closed them to a tight line and nodded.

"I won't be long."

She nodded again.

Zac laid a hand on her arm and gave it a light squeeze. "Stay down." He wanted to do more to reassure her, like take her in his arms, instead he released her and turned to work his way through the growth. He hadn't gone far before she disappeared from view. The foliage was thicker than a lot of jungles he'd been in. Still, even with caution, it

85

took him only two minutes to reach the road. Making sure it was clear, he crossed to the other side and into the trees, working his way back to where his truck should be.

∞

Skye watched Zac walk away and wanted to call him back — wanted to follow, but knew she needed to trust him. She trusted him more than any man she'd ever known.

Automatically her mind started to reach out to follow him. It took effort to keep it back. The want to be with him was very strong. Only reasoning that she needed to stay alert in the here and now stayed her. If she reached out, she would be vulnerable if something happened or someone came. Then she'd be no help to Zac.

Skye listened, trying to detect any sounds.

She couldn't believe he was there. It might not be fate, but he was a miracle to her. If anyone could save her, it was Zac Masters. Skye didn't doubt it, but it worried her, too. He was in danger because of her.

He was the type who would risk his life to do what was needed and what he felt was right. He'd been risking his life on operations so long it was second nature to him. It was what he did, but she still didn't want to see him in danger. Now he'd set himself up as her protector, she figured there was nothing she could say to change that.

Emotions hit her so hard it took her breath away. She didn't want Zac to see her as an assignment to protect but as a woman he might find interesting and wanted to be around. Reality hit her like a blow to the stomach, almost doubling her over. It wasn't likely to happen. Men didn't think of her that way, still the dream lingered in her heart. Again the wanting of him swept over her.

The image of Zac came to life in her mind. A series of scenes played out; Zac leading his men, keeping them safe while completing their mission. She saw him in the desert and jungle, black night, burning heat of the day, and sweltering humidity that stuck his shirt to his body, lining every muscle. The final image that came to her was of him in sleep. It had only been that morning. Skye wanted to discount it, that it wasn't real. Just a dream, but she knew better. She'd reached for him, called him and he'd come.

Her heart thundered at the possibility. She worried her bottom lips between her teeth. Had he really felt her? Had he felt her before?

Skye didn't know what to think but first things first. She had to prepare for Zac's return. The thought was hardly through her mind when the faint sound of a vehicle reached her.

Cஇஓ

Zac moved in. Directly across the road from his truck, he paused to watch the three men. He recognized the two from earlier. From Skye's description, the older, silver-haired man who shot at them would be Colonel Sterling. The tall, thin guy would be the other viewer, Wesley.

The third man he didn't have a name for but by the big, red tow truck hoisting the front end of his truck off the ground, his occupation was as obvious as the two flat tires. Zac watched the tow truck driver reach in his truck and turn on the emergency flashers.

"He'll show you where to park the truck." Sterling's voice reached him. "Just put it up on blocks. Take the two tires off and drop them back by later."

The tow truck driver came forward and looked closer at the driver's side tire. "There's no fixing this. It'll need new tires."

Sterling raised and lowered his head in acknowledgement. "Change them out and let me know the cost. I'll have it covered."

The tow truck driver leaned closer. "You know, this looks like a bullet hole." He looked back over his shoulder cautiously, as if judging the colonel.

Sterling met the man's gaze straight on for his lie. "Yeah, he lost it. He's been dealing with PTSD. He shot out his own tires. He's okay, now, back at the complex under house arrest. I'm sending him to one of the bases for some medical. I don't want this on his record though. It will cost him enough for the new tires. If you bring the bill with the tires, I'll have it paid then." There was a slight stress on the last words that invited no more comment.

The tow truck driver's hand came up to rub the back of his neck as he stared back at the tires a moment longer, then he looked up at the colonel. "I should have them sometime tomorrow," he said with his heavy Appalachian accent coming through.

"That'd be good."

Zac wondered if there was any way of reaching the driver. He started to edge closer to the road when the sound of another vehicle reached him. He pulled back into the brush.

Sterling glanced down the road then back to the man. "Wesley will ride back with you and show you where to leave the truck."

The driver took it as a dismissal and got in the tow truck, starting the motor as the thin man limped around to the passenger side. Zac knew he could make it to the truck and probably slip on to it without being noticed, but that would leave Skye alone, and he couldn't do that even long enough to go get help.

Zac watched helplessly as his truck, his cell phone, and gun pulled away. Frustration tasted sour in his mouth. The tow truck swung around, coming back right in front of him. Now was the time. He could make it. A quick dash out and pull himself on, but he couldn't do it. The certainty that Skye would be gone before he got back burned in him.

With nothing else to do about it, he turned his attention to the approaching black truck. A jacked up, fully decked-out model with windows tinted to the maximum legal limits. Instead of passing by like Zac figured, it slowed and pulled off the road by the colonel.

The engine cut off and a man, approximately his height and built, dressed similar to him in an olive green T-shirt, camo pants, and boots, stepped down. He spared a glance at the receding tow truck before turning his attention to Sterling. "Any trouble?"

Sterling shook his head. "He wondered but accepted the explanation. He won't make waves, at least until after we're gone but by then it'll be too late."

The man, who must be Coons, nodded. "We better get going then. That storm is moving in harder and stronger than they thought. They're already battening down the coast. We're supposed to be hit with some heavy rains starting sometime during the night."

"You think you can find her?" Sterling walked to the truck.

Even from the distance, Zac could see the malice in the sergeant's grin. "She's as good as got." He reached back into the cab and drew out a holster and fastened it on.

"See she's not to be hurt," Sterling said crossly.

"I'll see she's not damaged, but I won't promise there won't be a few chunks taken out of her hide. Found anything about the man with her?"

"Nothing much, but he's Army. There was a uniform in the truck. I'll look into it more when I get back to the office."

"Do you think she called him?"

"Don't know how. We closed down all the lines. They weren't working before she got into the lab."

"Dumb sap was in the wrong place. Women always get ya in trouble." The man chuckled.

Sterling shifted. "Make sure they never find his body."

"No problem." The man pulled a yellow wad of material from inside the cab then went around the back of the truck and lowered the tailgate.

A rush of unease hit Zac and he started to pull back even before the first howl echoed out of the truck.

Chapter Seven

"Ready to go to work?" Coons said.

A high-pitched K-9 whine sounded, adding more speed to Zac as he raced through the undergrowth. He had to get out of there before the dogs were released and picked up his scent. He needed to get to Skye and start wiping out their trail and setting down a new one before the dogs got close. It didn't give him a lot of time.

Things just got a lot more challenging. He wasn't worried about evading a couple men or even going in to take them out, but hounds, especially depending on how they were trained, were a whole new component in the equation. The hunt was definitely on.

Zac cut across the road, glancing briefly at the sky. Coons' words on the storm moving in came back to him. The sky was still clear blue but that could change awfully fast. He wondered if there was a way they could get out of the woods before nightfall which was only a couple hours away.

From the map he'd looked at earlier, they'd be close to five miles or more from the next intersecting road and probably ten to fifteen miles to a community. They were about as far in the middle of nowhere as they could get in the region. Rugged terrain and a storm coming in, not a great situation.

The image of soft, clear green eyes framed by long, flowing blonde hair came to his mind, and he gave thanks he was there. He would get Skye out of there. Zac didn't doubt his resolve. It was what he did and for once, it felt personal.

Zac let instinct guide him back. Closing in to the area he left her, he stopped and listened. He could detect no sound. "Skye," he called out in a hushed tone. A half minute passed and he was about to call again when he heard a rustling sound on his left and her head popped up twenty feet away. Relief showed on her face.

She burst from the bushes before he made it half way to her. She threw herself into his arms, knocking him back a step. Zac was more than willing to wrap his arms around her but she slipped free before he got a chance to. Color flamed into her cheeks, as she looked away.

"Sorry." She tilted her face down. "I got worried."

Zac reached for her, pulling her to him in a movement that surprised himself. He wasn't usually so forward with women, but he liked the feel of her against him, and more, it felt right.

Her head jerked up, eyes wide.

"Don't apologize." He growled the words out, wanting to say more, wanting to kiss her. Instead, he held her, studying her face as she did his. Her lips pulled up in a hint of a smile and she went lax in his arms, leaning into him slightly.

"Did you find your truck?" The words were breathy, but they steadied the situation.

"It was being towed away. I couldn't get close enough to get my phone."

"There's no cell service here anyway."

"We have a problem." He released her and stepped back. "I saw a man, my height, slightly thinner with a cruel streak."

"Coons," she gasped.

Alarm flashed in Zac. "Has he ever hurt you?"

"No. He acts like a good friend type, nothing

91

inappropriate, but he makes me uncomfortable."

Zac studied her, verifying the truth in her words. "Well, he just showed up with a couple dogs."

Skye inhaled sharply and went pale. "His dogs are hunters. He brags them up. That they can track anything. They won this big competition a year ago, but they got in a fight with another dog. They hurt the other dog so bad it had to be put down, and he can't compete anymore. He doesn't let anyone near them, not that I've ever wanted to try. They snarl, bark and jump against the fence if you even get close to them. I mean like several house lengths away. None of the men will even go near."

Zac caught her hand giving it a squeeze. "Don't worry about it."

"Can we out run them?"

"No. We're going to out think them. They aren't going to get close to us, but we've got to get moving. Stay right with me. Follow in my trail wherever I go. We're going to head back to that stream but we're going to be laying down some false trails on the way."

With that, Zac released her hand and headed off to the right about two hundred feet before stopping. "Okay, back track."

They made it to their starting point and he took off to the left again going between two to three hundred feet before turning her back. They followed their original path until Skye figured they were about halfway to the stream when Zac changed direction once more taking them through the growth in a different angle, going a little farther this time before backtracking.

They reached the stream and followed it to a spot where the trail curved around some bushes away from the bank which dropped off a couple feet to the water.

"Okay, this should work." Zac stopped studying the area.

"What are we going to do?" Skye tried to see what he

was thinking. She thought they were planning on getting in the stream and following it, but there was no way into the water.

"Jump down to the water. Land as close to the far side as you can get but staying in. I want you to try not to touch the ground on either side of the stream. Then I'll jump down after you and we'll follow the stream, letting it take our scent away.

"I don't know if I can make it to the water." Skye studied the distance, not questioning what he wanted.

"Don't worry, you can make it. Trust me. Just clear the bushes and your momentum will carry you the rest of the way. The biggest worry is the landing. The bottom of the stream doesn't look too rocky but it'll be slick."

She took a deep breath and nodded. "How do I do it?"

"Back up and take a running start. Jump and tuck your legs when you get about here. I promise, your momentum will carry you far enough into the water. Can you do it?"

Zac tried to gauge her reaction. He sensed her determination. Skye didn't shy away from things. She handled them. He liked that. There was also a touch of adventurer in her, though it seemed to have been tempered. What he was asking was a big leap of faith, literally.

Again she nodded and moved back about ten feet. Setting her jaw, Skye burst forward like she'd been set off by a starting gun. By the time she reached him, her stride was wide and her arms were pumping. She jumped, pulling her legs up and out into a position that a long jumper could be proud of, easily clearing the low brush on the edge of the bank.

For an instant, Zac was afraid she was going to go too far and clear the whole stream. Skye must have realized it also because at that moment she pulled out of her tuck and flailed her arms. She dropped, bending her knees with the impact, gasping as water splashed up drenching her, but she didn't cry out. Skye held her pose for several counts before she straightened, turned and beamed up at him.

"Good job." He smiled, took a couple steps back and made the jump, coming down beside her. "Let's go."

They stayed in the stream well beyond the point where their trail had angled back toward the road. It was a fallen log impeding their path that drove them out since there was no way under it or over it without touching and leaving their scent.

"We'll take a five minutes rest then pick up the pace." Zac broke the silence they'd been traveling in.

"I'm okay," she said quickly.

"You're more than okay. You're doing great, but it's better to rest while we can. You never know what's coming."

"Do you think the dogs will pick up our trail?"

"Yes. I'm hoping they'll follow my trail back to the road first. What we've done is buy us some time."

"So what do we do now?"

"Try to get out of here and find help before getting caught." He barely got the words out before the grin.

"I think I figured that part out," she said sourly but smiled back.

"That's the basis of the plan. Do you know this area?"

"Not really. I've never hiked it. I usually stick to the developed trails south of here on the other side of the installation."

"How far is the installation and town?"

She looked thoughtful for a moment. "The nearest town's at least fifteen miles. I would say two and a half to three miles to the installation. I'm not really sure. If you follow the road, probably three miles, but if you cut through like I did, I'd say just over two from here. We haven't been going straight from it, some's been kind of parallel, I think. I just don't know." Her words were heavy with apology.

"It's okay." When he felt her fingers curl around his,

he realized he'd taken hold of her hand. Her fingers were long, slim, and delicate. He ran his thumb over the back of her hand, marveling at the feel.

Wisps of hair danced around her face, stirred by the wind. Zac wanted to catch a lock and finger it to see if it was as soft as it looked but forced his attention skyward. A gray tint crept in the sky which wasn't due fully to the nearing of night fall. Zac could now make out the edges of rolling clouds in the distance.

"The storm's moving in," Skye said beside him, tension spiking in her voice. "I was hoping it wasn't going to get this far inland."

"They said we might get some rain." Zac tried to make light of it, as he glanced at the sky, but he had a feeling it was going to be a lot more than the weather people originally predicted. Something told him they were in for a full-blown storm. As if to prove his speculation, a gust of wind rushed through the trees bringing with it a chorus of creaks from the branches.

"Come on. We better get moving. I'd like to find some shelter."

"What about the dogs?"

"We'll worry about them if they find us. If we're lucky, they'll call them back and wait out the storm before coming after us." He tried to sound convincing but didn't really believe it. If Skye was right at the price they put on her, nine millions was an awful lot of incentive. Zac couldn't fathom it. It didn't bode well for her.

He just hoped the false trails were enough to throw them off. It should work with the dogs, but the sergeant, that was another problem. Depending on his training and if he stayed with the dogs, he could figure out what they'd done and get the dogs back on track. Time—it was what they were buying but really wasn't on their side.

ભ૪

Skye pressed to follow Zac up the slope. Her heart

pounded in her chest, and it wasn't all from fear. She thought she was in decent shape, but was ready to drop. For at least forty-five minutes they'd been moving at a pace which was barely under a run. She concentrated on Zac's back and putting one foot in front of the other. Humidity boiled in the air. Only the wind kicking up from the oncoming storm made it bearable.

Skye knew if she asked for a break, he would stop, but she'd caught the distance bay of a hound. It sounded like they were getting closer, or at least they'd picked up their new trail. Zac had kept them heading pretty much straight east. They'd crossed two more streams and gone up and down one hill pushing through a myriad of bushes and briars when there wasn't any other way to go. For that reason, Skye was glad she'd chosen to wear long pants that day. She wiped the perspiration off her brow.

Zac had started several bouts of conversation which Skye figured were as much to keep her mind occupied as to learn about her. She'd learned a lot about him though, and about his family. He was very close to his brother, though they were their own men. Still, their lives had paralleled, down to joining the Army, their service and both becoming Airborne Rangers. They both had also received engineering degrees and pretty much liked the same things. Zac said they got the engineering from their father, military from their grandfather, and common sense from their mother.

Zan had been released nearly five months earlier, taking medical leave with his other accrued leave. Skye knew full well about his medical leave. She shuddered at the thought.

"Zan married Marley about two months ago. She's in medical research, pharmaceuticals, trying to develop a wide-based flu cure." He gave a small laugh. "I like her. She's keeping Zan busy learning new things. She didn't grow up on a military base but a boarding school for brilliant kids and was the youngest one there. I guess she missed out on a lot of things. Zan says he's done more dancing in the last two months than he has in his whole life. She never got to go to school dances, not even the prom."

Skye winced. She'd really wanted to go to prom, but that was kind of out of the question when you didn't even go to school.

He glanced back at her and stopped. "You didn't either."

It wasn't really a question, still she shook her head. The answer wouldn't come out, not because of shortness of breath but a choke point that formed in her throat. A tightness banded in her chest making it difficult to even swallow.

His palm came up to cup her cheek. "Would you like to go dancing with me?"

The question surprised her. Skye wondered if she'd really heard it or if it was all wishful thinking, but he seemed to be waiting for an answer. "Yes." The word came out in an explosion of air that brought a smile to his lips.

"It's a date then." He leaned forward and kissed her. Briefly there and gone but like before left her tingling and her heart pounding.

He was about ten feet ahead when she had herself under control enough that she could follow. Skye raced to catch up to him.

"You know, when Zan met his wife, they had a trek through the woods a lot like this. No dogs, but an assault team on their tail."

At first Skye thought he was teasing her then realized he wasn't. "Why?"

"Marley discovered something she wasn't supposed to, that would have hurt or killed a lot of soldiers. She was trying to report it, and there were some that didn't want the information getting out. They tried to kill her and my brother when he tried to help her."

"Wow."

"It worked out. They got the information into the right hands, those behind it are in prison, and Zan got Marley. They both seem pretty happy with how it turned out."

A hound's bay echoed hauntingly in the wind rushing through the trees.

"They're closer." Skye jerked around.

"It's okay. We just have to pick up the pace."

She heard his answer but couldn't seem to pull her eyes from where the now constant call rolled over her. They weren't going to make it. What would the dogs do when they caught them? They needed her but what about Zac?

"Skye."

She jerked again when his hand clamped down on her arm pulling her around.

"Come on."

She shook her head. "They want me. Need me. They won't hurt me. You can−"

"Don't go any farther with that, or you're going to make me real mad." Anger boiled in his eyes like the clouds coming over the mountains. "I'm not leaving you. Got it?" He didn't wait for her to argue or even answer. "So are you going to move or do I have to carry you?" The image of him packing the diplomat through the jungle just days earlier came to mind. He'd do it. He'd carry her until he dropped.

"Go." She took off up the hill, leaving him following her.

Skye put all she had into her flight. Zac's presence behind her was marked by the faint stirring of leaves, silent like a huge panther moving through the jungle. It gave her strength. Her heart pounded in her ears wiping out the dogs' constant chorus.

The top of the hill loomed just ahead. Fifty feet, forty, twenty, ten. She dug deeper, pushing for more. Skye burst out on top and almost went over as the ground dropped away into the ravine. She felt her feet go out from under her as she teetered over the edge.

Chapter Eight

Seconds held frozen as Skye was extended out in mid-air over the two hundred foot drop to the boulders below. Her stomach rolled. Then with single jerk, she landed back on the ground at Zac's feet.

He dropped down beside her, his hand still locked on the backpack strap which he'd snagged to keep her from going over.

Skye peered down and gulped in air, knowing the fall would have killed her. Finally, able to drag her gaze from the chasm, she looked at him. "That would have been a long first step." She reached inside herself for relief.

"I don't think you would have liked the landing." He opened his arms to her and she dove in, pressing into his chest as the first shudder raced through her.

He pulled her close, burying her face in his neck. His large hands slid over her back in comforting strokes that drew her even tighter. His heart beat thundered under her ear. Her heart settled into a matching rhythm.

"I've got to keep better track of you." His words rumbled through her, then she felt his lips on her neck, and she forgot about everything but him. His hand came up to frame her head and he eased her back. His eyes reached down into her, catching her secrets and heart, claiming all.

There was no thought of resistance when his head dipped, and he captured her mouth just as he did the rest of her. With each kiss he seemed to claim more of her, and with this, Skye gave herself fully to him. He devoured her and gave her strength in return. Her trembling had shifted from fear to desire when he ripped his lips from hers.

Zac stood abruptly, shoving his hands over his hair. "I have to stop this."

Skye about asked him why but he answered first.

"I have to think, keep a clear head to get us out of here." His gaze dropped back to her. "And all I can think of is you're mine, as if you don't have enough to be scared about."

Skye swallowed. "I'm not scared of you."

His eyes burned with intensity, but whatever he was going to say was cut off this time by a low howl that echoed through the woods. He glanced over his shoulder then back at the ravine. "How are you with climbing?"

"What?" It was her turn to stand and glance down the drop off she almost went over.

"We don't have much option," Zac said as he opened his backpack. "We can't backtrack now. The dogs are too close. We also can't out run them, and I'd just as soon not tangle with them unless I have to."

The image of sharp teeth tearing into him came to her. Skye didn't want that either. "I've done a little climbing, no repelling."

"Good because I don't have enough rope for that, just seventy-five feet of emergency line. See that ledge down there? I have enough rope to get you there. I want you to climb to that. I'll tie you off on me so, in case you fall, I can lower you."

"What about you?" Skye shoved down the nervousness that coursed through her.

"I can climb it."

The strength in his words encouraged her. She nodded, not that there was any alternative.

Zac dropped a rope on the ground. She picked it up and undid the knot. Wrapping it around her waist, she tied a bowline. When she looked up, she found him watching her, she grinned.

He reached out and gave the rope a tug. "Nice."

She shrugged. "It's one of the only knots I know along with the half hitch, square and granny."

"It's a good one to know. Ready?"

Skye couldn't help but glance over the drop again.

A large hand caught her chin and turned her back to face him. "I won't let you fall." The promise rumbled from deep within him.

Skye found herself trapped in his ice-blue eyes. There was no coldness in them. They burned with certainty and something more she wasn't sure she could name. She wondered if it was possible he could care for her in this short time.

"I've already fallen." The words slipped free without her realizing it until his lips kicked up at the corners.

"That's good to know. We'll talk more about that later. For now, over the side."

Skye stepped closer to the edge and looked over again, swallowing hard. She thought of herself as an adventurous person, but it was a long way down, easily five times the height of anything she'd ever attempted before.

"Skye, look at me!" Zac's demand jerked her around. He sat on the ground, the rope wrapped around his back, held in gloved hands on either side of him. "I'm not going to let you fall."

"I know." She breathed out.

"Take hold of the rope and don't look down. Ease to the edge, eyes on me. Lean back on the rope. Good. Keep your feet shoulder width apart and out against the rock. You're going to just walk down until you get to the ledge. Then, I'll climb down to you."

She nodded.

"Okay, look at your feet and step back."

Skye leaned back and stepped over the edge. Her life,

like her heart, hung in the hands of a man she'd met only a couple hours earlier. Funny thing was, she didn't doubt him with either.

⋙⋘

Zac felt his own breath catch. Skye's eyes came up to meet his. Trust crossed the space. She showed more confidence than many recruits he'd seen on their first rappels. The rope fairly slid through his fingers as he released it in a constant flow that wouldn't hang her up. He concentrated on the tension, watching for any sign of trouble.

Her words flirted across the back of his mind. 'I've already fallen.' He didn't doubt the words because he could've repeated and meant them. He just didn't know how they could be true. They'd just met, but he felt he'd known her for a long time, maybe forever. Certainly well over a year ... two, he amended. She'd been on the fringes of his mind at least that long.

He'd been dating June, and it was the month of June. His team had been sent on a mission. He could remember it clearly. The stirring he'd felt across his senses. When he got back, he'd gone out with June and ended the evening early. It felt wrong being with her. He'd felt disloyal. Since then, no woman had held his interest other than the one whose life literally slid through his hands.

A sharp, nerve-chilling howl cut the air. Zac glanced over his shoulder. The cry was close. He bit down on the urge to hurry Skye. She was doing well, and he didn't want to make her anxious and have an accident. The bay of one dog was picked up by the other making an eerie chorus that rolled up the hill behind him.

"I'm on the ledge." Skye voice floated up as the line went slack. Not taking time to untie the rope, Zac pulled on his backpack and scooted forward, shifting onto his stomach as he slid over the edge. He locked on to handholds as he searched for a place for his feet.

The first hound crested the rise. Feral, yellow-brown eyes in a bristled face flashed as it caught sight of him. The dog leapt the distance, going for his throat.

Zac's feet found hold and he lowered himself so that the fangs met open air just above his head. Skye's cry reached up from below him, but Zac focused on finding another handhold as the second dog joined the first, coming in lower, going for his wrist. Teeth scraped over his leather glove as Zac released his hold on the rock. Zac felt it catch, but pulled free before the jaws could clamp down.

Teeth bared, the dog strained forward after him to the point Zac thought it was going to go over the edge in its frenzy to reach him. He concentrated on the climb as rocks and dirt peppered him, along with the frustrated baying from the hounds denied their prey.

The climb wasn't as difficult as he feared because there were plenty of hand and foot holds. Still, it took several minutes to reach Skye and the ledge. Her hand brushed his back before he release his last hold and settled down beside her. He turned to her in time to catch the rush of air that escaped her with relief.

"You're okay." A trembling hand touched his cheek, caressing its way down to his neck. Her eyes drifted closed, and she wavered slightly. Zac reached for her, afraid she'd fall. At his touch, her eyes shot open. She dove for him, pressing him back against the rock, her face into his neck as shudders racked her body.

To his surprise and disappointment, she only remained a few seconds before she drew back. "I'm sorry. The dogs … I thought … so close." Her hand covered her mouth, cutting off the flow of words as she managed a couple deep breaths before expelling. "Sorry," she said again. "I'm okay. "It's just−"

"That was close," he finished for her. He glanced up. One of the muzzles could be seen hanging over the edge as the dogs continue their racket. "We've got to get going."

He looked below, calculating if they had enough rope for her to reach the bottom. Estimating they'd be about twenty feet short he picked a point about halfway down. It wasn't as wide as the spot they were on but it would be sufficient. "There's our next point."

Skye nodded, not hesitating on taking a handhold on the rock. Zac set himself with the rope once more around his back so he could easily let it out. "Ready?"

"Yes."

"Go."

She started down the cliff. It seemed like hardly any time passed before she called up that she was there. He followed her, taking a fraction longer than she had to reach the point. Still it seemed longer. If he had the ropes he needed, he could have rappelled in seconds. Still, they were making good time. He just hoped it would be enough.

"Last leg," he said reaching her. He settled right into position to belay her without giving any time for comment.

○ॐ○

Skye took her cue leaning back against the rope as soon as he said "ready".

It was easier stepping into air this time, then again she was only about forty feet from the bottom now. Still, she liked the thrill it gave her. The hardest thing was ignoring the continual baying of the hounds. The sound grated on her nerves. She wished for some way to quiet them but there was only one person who could do that.

Silence ripped across the canyon so abruptly Skye jerked. Her attention shot up and she missed her footing. Twisting on the rope, she slammed into rock. A shriek slipped out as she felt herself drop. She only dipped a couple feet with the stretch of the rope before she smacked back into the cliff again.

"Skye!" Zac shouted as she fought for a hold to keep herself righted.

"I'm okay," she yelled up. "I just slipped. The dogs."

"Don't worry about them, just go." She heard the urgency in his voice. Swallowing hard, she pulled first one foot up and pressed it against the rock wall then the other. A touch of nerves hit her as she released the rock, moving her hands back to the rope. She swallowed to moisten her throat. "Okay. Let out the rope."

Just as Skye reached the bottom, a rock dislodged from above, clattering its way down the face, bringing a shower of pebbles with it before landing not far from her. Once more, she jerked, looking up. The face leaning over at the top sent more terror than the bristly faces with sharp canines, even when they were snapping down at Zac.

Sergeant Coons peered over the edge. Sterling's head joined his. Dark clouds seemed to roll around them.

"Zac." Her warning was unneeded.

"Untie the rope." The directive was followed by the rest of the rope being dropped down to land just behind her. Zac already had a handhold and was starting his climb down. The only sign he showed of acknowledging the men's presence was the rapidness of his pace.

Skye worked on the knot, her attention continually going to the top of the cliff. Her fingers trembled making her fumble, but finally it dropped free. She looked up again to see Coons leaning a little farther over the edge, his arm extended out. His arm jerked as the gun in his hand kicked.

Skye jumped at the crack echoing down in the ravine.

Dirt burst up not far from Zac. He didn't even break in his movement, but she had to clamp a hand over her mouth to keep from screaming. The next shot missed Zac and the rock wall burying in the ground not far from her.

She heard Sterling snap at Coons about firing so close to her, and it gave her an idea. Taking a half-dozen steps to the side, she put herself directly under Zac. Hoping she'd be a deterrent from shooting him in fear of hitting her.

When no more shots came, she decided it worked. The two men disappeared from view. Grabbing up the end of the rope, she held it in her hand and looping down around her elbow then back up like her father had taught her to wrap. She'd just got it all up and was tying it off when a movement on the cliff top caught her attention.

Coons had moved along the cliff a good fifty feet to the side, giving him a different angle.

"No!" The cry escaped her at the same time the shot sounded. Eight feet above her, Zac flinched as the bullet ricocheted just over his head. He pushed off, releasing his hold. Another shot hit where he'd been a second earlier. Skye gasped as he dropped next to her.

ભૈ

Years of training had taught Zac how to land. He took the impact easily. Coming out of his crouch, he opened his arms, scooping Skye with him as he dove for the bottom of the cliff. Pressing her into the rock, he wrapped one arm over her head, sheltering her with his body.

His heart still bounded from the move she'd made to put herself in direct line of fire if they tried for him. He wanted to shake her. He wanted to yell at her. He wanted to kiss her.

All he could do was wait until the man above came to his senses and realized he was as apt to hit her as him. Then he and Skye could sneak away into the undergrowth that lay as a taunting shelter a few feet away. It ended up he didn't have to wait long.

"Stop, you might hit her." The words carried down from above.

Not willing to trust them, Zac remained still, flattening his body to Skye's. Her breaths stirred the nerve endings on his neck. The soft fruity fragrance of her filled his alert senses, threatening to distract him. It took all his force of will to remain focused for any hint of danger above. As tight as they were to the rock, he didn't think there was any way they could be seen from up above.

Skye shifted. Fingers tenderly closed on his bicep.

He glanced down at her.

"Are you all right?" He felt the words as much as heard them.

"Yes, except that you scared a couple years off my life when you moved into their line of fire." He sounded gruff but didn't care.

"You're bleeding."

He followed her gaze to his arm where there was a smudge of blood.

"Just a scratch," he brushed it away as insignificant. "Probably a rock chip. Believe me, it's nothing. We need to get out of here. The dogs can't reach us, but I don't want to hang around if the men try. When I give the word, we make a break for the growth. Stay right behind me. Don't stop for anything. Understand?"

Skye nodded, and he didn't doubt her. She'd done everything he'd asked of her without question. She was amazing in her complete trust. He wanted to tell her that and a lot more, just now was not the time and definitely not the place. He slid his hand down her arm to lock around her fingers, giving them a little squeeze. "Ready?"

She nodded.

"Go," he said softly, turning and pulling her with him into a dash for the woods. Whether because they took them by surprise or the fact that Skye was behind him and they couldn't get a clear shot of him without endangering her, they made it into the trees without any gunfire following them.

Their pace slowed out of necessity because of the foliage and rocks. Zac was forced to release her hand to catch branches to keep them from whipping back at her. He pushed for a rapid as possible pace over the rough terrain until they'd covered what he figured was well over a half mile before he pulled up to rest. Zac smiled, looking back at her.

Skye gulped in air, hugging the coiled rope to her like

it was still her lifeline.

"I can take that now." He reached for it, swinging his backpack off his shoulders.

"Do you think they're after us?"

He looked up and shook his head. "I bet they headed back. I don't know what kind of climbers either are. Coons might have made it down the cliff, but the colonel wasn't dressed for it, and I didn't see any sign that they had a rope."

"I never heard them talk about climbing."

"We don't have long until the storm is going to hit, and it's almost dark. I'm betting they'll wait it out, return better equipped, and try to pick up our trail with the dogs."

"Can we go on?" Apprehension filled her words.

He looked up again. "Not much longer."

Long shadows filled the valley the ravine had dumped them in. Wind whipped through the trees. The sky darkened, not only from the coming night, but the approaching storm.

"We better start looking for a place to wait out the night." Zac took stock of their surroundings.

"What about the storm?" Skye labored to catch her breath.

"We'll need shelter from it, if we can find some. This area's riddled with caves."

"The trick will be finding one that isn't already occupied by a critter that isn't of a mind to share."

He smiled at her. "You know, you don't have much of an accent, but every once in a while it does come through."

She blushed.

"I like it. It's kind of cute. Come on let's go."

She watched him take a few steps before she followed. *Cute, that's not quite what I wanted him to think. At least it wasn't freak.* She tried for the positive but only felt marginally better.

The first drop of rain lit on her cheek as she hurried to

catch him. She glanced up nervously. Clouds boiled over the ridge to the east and rolled down at them. Wind picked up with more force, slamming her in the face, snagging away her breath, and plastering her clothes to her body. Branches creaked overhead. Fear spiked within her, then Zac was there catching her hand once more.

"Come on, this way." He led her through the trees. Rain pattered on the leaves above. If they didn't find shelter soon, they'd be drenched. The rumbling of thunder rolled through the clouds.

"There."

Skye barely made out the word before it was carried away by the wind. She looked to where Zac pointed. Trees parted ahead. In the faint, remaining light, she could just make out a small pool of water nestled at the bottom of the hillside. A rock slab cantilevered out over the water. There was a little cove and, on one side, a bank protected the space under it. The area couldn't quite be called a cave but it was sheltered. The relief she felt seeing it eclipsed the amazing beauty of the spot.

Zac headed down the steep slope toward the stream that flowed out of the pool.

Skye followed, slipping and sliding down part way on her bottom. Her legs trembled as she regained her footing.

"I don't think there's any way behind it. We're going to have to cross here," he said. "It'll be nothing after your last leap."

The narrowest part of the stream was at least four feet across and there was no running room because of rocks and trees. To her, the distance looked immense. Whether it was that they were so close to a place they could rest, or the approaching night, Skye felt totally sapped of strength. She drew in a deep breath, but it did nothing to relieve her apprehension.

"I'll go first," Zac said, obviously picking up on her hesitation. He made the jump easily.

Skye stared down at the space and water which grew darker and more ominous as she stared. She swallowed. Her heart pounded. She honestly wasn't sure she could make it. Raising her gaze, she looked at Zac standing patiently with the rain drizzling down on him.

He held out his hand in silent encouragement. Skye reached out to him, but it was wide enough they couldn't touch. Longing hit her stronger than the trepidation. She took a step and jumped. Clearing the water, her foot came down on the edge of the bank. She teetered, her muscles screaming in protest as she fought to steady herself. For a moment, she thought she had it then fatigue slammed in on her again and her legs went out from under her.

Skye felt herself drop, and she had no more strength to stop it, then a band of muscle snagged her around the waist, hauling her forward. Weakly, she sagged against the strong chest, aware of the heartbeat thundering under her ear. She floated as security seeped into her. Skye closed her eyes and let it take her.

Chapter Nine

Panic hit Zac as Skye started to slip from the bank. He knew she'd been to the brink of her endurance, moving on adrenaline and will-power, but she'd seemed to pull it together when she made the jump. Only the fact he had been prepared to catch her, had let him keep her from dropping into the water. Her body went limp against him.

Normally, he'd have hoisted a person up over his shoulder in a fireman's carry, but he couldn't with her. Sliding one arm down behind her thighs, he lifted her, cradling her to him. Her head lulled against his shoulder, her long hair spilling down over his arm. For a second, he could only stare down at her as her soft beauty touched his heart. She was amazing, and she was worn out. He pulled himself back into line.

Careful not to jar her crossing the rocky ground, he made his way around the pool. Using his body to shelter her, he pushed through the shrubs blocking the path. Up against the lee of the hillside, the little cove was surprisingly affective at cutting the wind along with the rain.

He leaned her against the back wall, slipped off his backpack, and removed the thin, silver emergency blanket from a pocket. Opening it, he laid it on the dry ground, covering the layer of fine, silky dirt. He removed the backpack Skye had been carrying all day and settled her on the blanket, folding it over her. It wasn't cold yet, but he didn't want to risk the chance of her getting chilled.

She sighed and stirred. Her eyes fluttered open. She looked up bewildered. "A dream," she breathed out.

"Skye." He brushed her cheek with his knuckles when her eyes started to close.

"Why are you always only in my dreams?" she said before going back to sleep.

Zac contemplated on waking her but saw no reason not to let her rest while he got their shelter set for the coming night. There wasn't much light left to work by. Wood was the first priority before it became too wet. It didn't take him long to gather a pile that would easily carry them through the night, and the next day, if needed. It also didn't take long to get a small fire going. Next, he filtered water to refill their bottles.

He glanced at Skye. She slept peacefully, in the exact position he'd lowered her. Her beautiful face peaceful, framed by her golden locks that even damp beckoned his fingers. Again, he contemplated waking her, to get her to eat something, but it was obvious her body needed rest more. He dug in his pack and pulled out a snack bar, leaving the MREs, meals ready to eat, stored there until Skye was awake to eat with him. Luckily, he always kept a two-day supply of the food packs plus a couple spares.

He debated a second on going through her pack, then deciding they were in this together, and that he needed to know the full extent of their supplies, he opened the first small pocket. It didn't hold much, a couple pens, mints and eight dollars and some change. The next pocket held a small, travel sized first-aid kit with the minimum stuff. There were personal items, tissues, a reasonably good pocket knife, a lighter and small LED flashlight with a couple extra batteries. Her emergency supplies. At least she had some. That was better than most people.

The larger pocket yielded more. Her purse was on top. He set it aside, leaving it for last. He found a nice quality wind breaker, a bag of assorted, small-sized candy bars, homemade chocolate chip cookies that were a little crushed, but considering what they'd been through were in surprisingly good shape. She also had a handful of granola bars and a box of energy drink power mixes to go in water. In the bottom of the bag was a small, light-weight throw, made of soft material with tasseled edges. Zac looked at the find, all in all, not bad. With what he had, they'd easily be okay for several days, if it took them that long to walk out.

Normally, he wouldn't think it would be that big of a challenge, but something told him it wouldn't be easy, and not all due to the storm.

He turned his attention back to Skye. Nine million dollars, he shook his head. It was unbelievable, but he didn't doubt. The men's actions definitely confirmed it, though he wouldn't have doubted her anyway.

Lightning lit the sky. Darkness had closed around them like a blanket while he'd been contemplating their situation. He might as well start fixing up some dinner. Randomly, he pulled out a MRE. He wasn't too picky about them, and all that were in his backpack were ones he didn't mind eating.

Lightning flashed again, followed immediately with a crack of thunder. It was the scream that echoed it that made him jump and twist around. Skye sat up in the silver blanket, her eyes wide open in terror.

He relaxed, shifting to his knees. "Skye," he said softly.

She gulped in air. When she turned to him. She visibly relaxed. "How did I?" She let the question drop off.

"I carried you. You collapsed. We should have rested more. You need to tell me when you need a break."

"I…" she nodded. "The storm's picking up."

"Yes." The rain now poured down. "Are you hungry?"

"Yes. I have a couple granola bars, some cookies and candy." She pushed back the blanket.

"I know I found them." He motioned behind him where he'd been taking stock. "They'll be good for dessert but I have something with a higher nutritional intake." He pulled out two of the MREs. "You know what they are?"

She smiled, then laughed. "I've heard some of the guys talk about them but never had one. Are they as bad as they sound?"

"Some are. Some are quite good. I only stock the ones I think are good, so you're in luck."

"Fine dining tonight, then." She scooted over by him. Her lips twitching in hints of a smile.

He handed her a water bottle. "Here, drink this first."

"Thank you."

He made sure she downed it while he heated the food.

"What can I do to help?"

"Just relax. You're in charge of dessert," he added before she could object. "I have some cookies, too. The mother of one of my men made them. I'd dropped a package off to her for him. That's how I ended up this way."

"They say no good deed—" She shrugged.

"I'm not complaining."

"That's because you go into ugly situations all over the world to rescue people." Lightning filled the sky, drawing her attention. "What do we do, now?"

"Rest and wait it out. We're safe for now."

She fell quiet for a moment. "Zac, I'm sorry you got caught up in this."

"It's okay."

Her eyes were watery when she looked at him. "You've lost your truck, been ran all over the hills, and shot at."

He put down the packet of food he was stirring and came up on his knees, settling directly in front of her. When her face tilted down, he placed his hand under her chin raising it back up so she met his gaze. "I can replace my truck, and it wasn't the first time I've been shot at. I wouldn't want to be anywhere else than here with you."

She gave what sounded like a cross between a laugh and a hic-up. "Not on a beach somewhere?"

The image of her stretched out on the sand in a swimsuit with the sun shining down on her came to mind. "With this storm?" he asked lightly. "It's not really beach weather. We'd be swept off the sand. I'm good where I'm at." He glanced over his shoulder. "Campfire, hot meal waiting, a beautiful girl, a rainfall serenade to set the mood. What more could a guy ask for?"

"Not to be shot at."

"Just adds to the excitement." He tried to brush her concern aside. What he wanted to do was take her in his arms and kiss her fears away. "How about something to eat?" He shifted back to the meal packs that were now ready.

"Great, I'm starving."

"Well, this is ham steak. It should fill you up and is pretty good."

"I could eat anything. Breakfast was a long time ago."

He handed her the meal, picked up him own, and took several bites.

"Not bad," she said after the first bite, after a couple more, she sighed and slowed.

"Told you." He glanced her way. "When did you start running?"

She stilled. "It seems like forever ago. This morning, right after breakfast. I was already planning on leaving then."

"You said your car wouldn't start?"

She nodded. "Someone messed with it."

"You're certain?" With all that had happened, he wanted the facts.

"I found the line they cut. They didn't even try to be tricky and hide it."

"So you'd been running several hours before you ran into me."

She nodded. "I figured my only chance was to make it to the road and hopefully flag someone down. That didn't work very well." She scoffed. "All I did was get you pulled into this."

"I told you, I'm not complaining."

"Why not?" Skye tilted her head to the side studying him, trying to see into him. She knew what made him the way he was, or at least thought she did, but this seemed even more than his sense of honor.

"Because I think I'm supposed to be involved." His answer was simple but his eyes were intense. "You called me."

"I … I." Skye wasn't sure what to say, but he continued.

"You walked into my dream last night." He waited a fraction, giving her time to deny, but she didn't, because she couldn't.

She remembered. She'd seen him sleeping, and had the urge to touch him, calling out for help. Skye shook her head. "No one's ever known I'm there before. I'm not really there." Her pulse picked up as he watched her.

"I knew." The words were firm, full of certainty.

She shook her head again, the possibility that just seemed too unbelievable.

"I've known for a long time when you were there. When you were watching." His eyes burned in their intensity. "My Skye watcher."

She jerked at the term in which she thought of herself, but no one else had ever used it. "You really knew I was there?" Her heart pounded.

"Yes. I kept feeling something, a brush against my senses, an awareness."

"As far as I know, no one else ever has. Though being twins probably made you more perceptive to me, I don't think your brother ever knew." Her mind went over the possibilities. "I'm sure he never picked me up."

Zac shrugged. "You weren't for him." He leaned forward and pressed his lips to hers.

Skye gasped and pulled back. "You kissed me."

"I did it earlier today and you didn't seem to mind." He stared deep into her eyes, searching for the answer to that. "I plan to do it again."

"I don't freak you out?"

"No!" He kissed her again, hard and deep.

Skye returned the kiss, going weak against him.

"Wow." He breathed out when he came up for air. "Do you kiss every guy like that?"

"No," she said weakly, trying to get herself under control.

"Good. Because if that's how you do, you're going to get yourself in trouble."

"I've never kissed any guy like that."

"Never?" For the first time she detected doubt in his words.

She shook her head. Feeling self-conscious, she pulled away, looking out at the rainy night.

He remained quiet a minute before he laid a hand on her arm.

After a moment, she swallowed and looked back. "I don't have a lot of experience kissing." She took several more bites of food, wishing he'd say something or she could change the subject but for some reason she felt compelled to explain.

"I kissed two boys in school, but they were an experiment more than anything, brief and not great. In the last couple years, there were only three other guys. The first guy I started to make friends with and liked, the Colonel sent away. The second, the colonel asked him to keep me happy. I was thinking of quitting the program and leaving. Number three was trying to tick-off the Colonel. It succeeded, and he was transferred, but I'd already figured out what he was up to. After that, I kind of gave up on guys."

"How'd you figure out the last guy?" Concern furrowed his brow, then he smiled. "You peeked on him."

She shrugged, taking another mouthful of food, not feeling guilty about being caught. "There used to be an older guy here, killing time until he retired, and he warned me to be careful. I'd already kind of figured out the guy was a user. He had a girl in town and one back home. He was pretty full of himself and bragging that he could get any girl he wanted, including me."

"So you can hear conversations beside see. I didn't know that was possible."

"No." Now she did blush. Luckily, in the dark, she didn't think he could see. "I'm fair at reading lips."

"You're kidding."

She shook her head. "I've never told anyone but Marta."

"Who's Marta?"

"She was a secretary at the installation, and my mother's best friend, but she was more like a grandmother to me. She took me in after my parents died. Ran interference and tried to temper Sterling's control over me."

"Where is she now?"

"She died. So Sterling got his wish. I stayed around because I didn't have anywhere else to go."

"You said you were going to leave. Where were you going to go?"

She shrugged again, looking once more out into the dark, stormy night, setting the food aside, no longer hungry. "I didn't really know. West."

"All the way west to California?"

She looked over giving him a half-smile. "Don't worry. I don't expect you to take over care of me."

He reached up and brushed a knuckle against her cheek. "I wasn't thinking of it quite that way. More like, maybe we see where this connection between us is supposed to head. You can't deny there is one." The hand on her cheek opened as he slid it back to bury it into her hair, drawing her to him. The action was slow, giving her plenty of time to pull away if she wanted.

Skye wanted nothing more than to be kissed by him again. She trembled at the first touch. The air in her lungs caught. His lips were warm and firm like before. The taste of him before had tantalized her and then it was gone. This time the kiss was slow, letting her savor. When she touched his neck with trembling fingers, his arm slid around her waist, drawing her closer. He held her tight, but Skye knew instinctively at any sign of protest he'd release her.

His mouth moved over hers in patient tutoring strokes. She followed. An absolute rightness settled through her. She knew this man. He was the one who'd always been on the fringes of her mind. The one she'd been waiting for to find her and hadn't even known she'd been waiting.

Zac broke from her mouth, breathing hard. His gaze roaming her face, as if he too was taking her in, and trying to believe she was real and not a dream that was going to slip away. His hands framed her face, his thumb stroked over her lips. Skye kissed it.

The corner of his lips turned up. "You know, you're a fast learner."

"I keep expecting to wake up."

"And when you do, I'll still be here. But for now, I think it would be a good idea if we both get some sleep. We don't know what tomorrow will bring."

"Do you think they'll come after us?" Dread seeped back in.

"They have to. They're already committed. They tried to kill me and made a deal with some people they don't want to cross. There's no walking away from it for them.

The when, depends on the storm. So we'll have to be prepared."

"You make it sound simple."

"It is. We need to keep a clear head, so that means I shouldn't kiss you anymore because when I do, all I can think about is you, and I need to be alert and observant. That also means getting rest while we can." He handed her the throw from her backpack. "We'll settle down back there."

He motioned to the silver blanket she woke up in. She also noticed he'd said we. Skye hoped that meant he would be close to her, like maybe hold her. She wanted that. For once in her life she really didn't want to be alone. She just didn't know how to ask him if he would mind being close enough she could touch him without sounding pathetic.

Skye glanced back at him before going to the blanket and stretching out on it.

His attention remained focused on finishing his food, then cleaning up and repacking their packs. The last thing he picked up was the bag of cookies. He looked to her. "You forgot your dessert."

Her heart fluttered as he took one, stood and walked to her. Instead of dropping to the ground beside her, he extended the cookie down. As soon as she took it he moved off, settling on the ground, leaning back against the wall a good six feet away.

Her heart fell, then she chided herself. Had she really believed he'd settle down beside her, take her in his arms, and hold her close? She was so foolish. She knew better.

She wasn't the type of girl that inspired those kind of thoughts. She was Spook. That was the reason she depended so strongly on herself. It didn't matter what Zac said about her being meant for him, and that he'd kissed her. Whatever it was that drew men, she definitely didn't have it.

The problem was whenever she looked at him, she

believed that maybe there was someone for her – no, not someone – Zac was the man she wanted.

The food in her stomach turned to lead, and the air thickened to sludge. What created the link between them letting him know of her presence? Was it all because she wanted him so badly? Had she forced or created the bond?

Tears started to well up, threatening to break free. Hurriedly, she took a bite of cookie then choked on it. Zac was beside her in an instant with a water bottle in his hand.

"You okay?" he asked when she finally managed to quit coughing.

"Yeah, just swallowed wrong." She brushed at tears that had more to do with the ache in her heart than choking.

C380

Silently, Zac eyed her. Didn't Skye have any idea how expressive she was? Something had come over her and it wasn't coughing. When he kissed her, she'd flowed with wonder and pleasure. She'd been so open, it was heart stopping. Then in a split second she'd closed down.

Had one of those men hurt her more than what she'd made it sound? He hoped not, because what he'd said about Zan not being for her went double for any other man. She was his. He didn't know how he could be so certain of it, but he was.

The problem was she was so young and innocent, it scared him. She knew what he did, he tried to reason with himself. She'd seen it. But he had done it. That had been his life.

No matter that he'd done it for good and upheld honor the best he could, he'd been in a lot of dark places and tough situations. Men died around him, some at his hands. He pushed the thoughts away.

Firelight glistened off moisture on her cheek making her look even more vulnerable. He wanted to pull her into his arms and hold her. But that wasn't what she needed out of him. She needed the protector, the clear-headed man that

122

got things done, no matter the odds.

Would she really want the man behind that person when all was said and done? Was he just deluding himself she was for him? To her, he was an airborne ranger, a man of action, but that was in the past, at least it would be once he had her safe. Then he'd just be a normal guy, a nerdy engineer.

The teasing some of the guys used to give him came back. "Why you wasting all your time on math and junk? There are women waiting out there."

The razing hadn't bothered him. He'd liked the challenge to his mind, thrived on it as much as he'd thrived on the challenge of ranger training to his body. And as for women, he only wanted one, this one. He wondered if he'd known she'd been waiting back then. He shook his head. That didn't make sense. She'd been just a kid.

Lightning spilt the sky, filling every inch of their shelter with its flash. She jumped but didn't look up at him. He needed her to look at him. "Skye." When he touched a finger to her chin, she tipped her head farther to the side, away from him.

Zac jerked his hand back. "I won't hurt you." The words tore from him.

"I know." A haunting whisper drifted to him.

She started to glance his way then shifted back.

The ache in him expanded. "Skye," he said again. This time when he put pressure on her chin, her head came up. Even in the flickering light, there was no missing the tears glistening in her eyes. They tore at him.

"Sweetheart." All his good intensions of giving her space evaporated. "What is it?" He wrapped his arms around her and felt her resist for the briefest second then she pressed her face into his chest.

"I'm so sorry." Her words were muffled against him but carried too much pain to be missed.

"It's all right." He held her close, running one hand up

and down her back, trying to soothe her.

"I didn't mean to."

Confusion took over everything within him. "Didn't mean to what?"

She shook her head. "I'm so sorry. I just wanted to love you."

For a moment, he thought he heard her wrong, but his heart caught on 'love you' and soared. He replayed them over and over – love you. "That's nice to know because I love you."

That had her shaking her head, trying to break free. "No, no you don't." She sprang to her feet and darted toward the curtain of rain.

Chapter Ten

He caught her just before she dashed out into the dark torrent. "Skye!" He pulled back, wrapping his arms around her. Her body trembled against him, but this time it wasn't desire or even fear.

"Sweetheart." He pressed his lips to her temple.

She tried to turn away then ruined her escape by dropping her head to his chest. "You don't see. It's not real. I created it."

Her face came up. Tears streaked her cheeks as agony pounded out of her like the rain just inches away. "I didn't know that I was or that I could. I just knew seeing you over time that I was falling in love with you. You were my own secret dream. I thought I was keeping you in my heart. I didn't know I was pressing those feelings on to you."

It took a second to pick up an understanding of her rambling. When it finally sank in what she was saying, it about knocked him over. "You think you created the bond between us?" Only his hands on her arms kept her from sinking to the ground in her obvious misery. Sorrow weighed her down, like none of the things she had faced that day.

"I'm so sorry, I—"

"No." He cut her off. "You didn't force this feeling into me. Understand. I've know it for a long time."

"But, what if it is not real?" She cried. "The connection is my fault. I invaded your dreams. I set this up.

I didn't mean to. It was just that you, I, you seemed to draw me in. I shouldn't have."

"But you couldn't stop because I did draw you."

Her head dropped to his chest. She nodded, and sagged against him. "I should have fought it. I just never knew you'd know. You were just my dream. My secret love."

"What if you're mine?"

Her head jerked up, her eyes searching his face for the truth. "How can you say that?"

"Because you are. I love you."

"Guys don't fall in love like that."

"Don't they? You've had that much experience to know?"

She made such a sour expression, he almost laughed. Oh, but she was expressive. He'd never have to wonder what she was thinking.

"I don't have any experience, but I've heard the guards talking."

That did bring out a laugh.

"What?"

"You little eavesdropper. You heard them talking to each other. Guys don't admit emotions to other guys. When they talk about women, it's usually for one-up-manship." He cradled her head in his hands, stroking the taunt muscles at the base of her neck. She melted into his hands, sagging into him.

Pleasure hummed through him in response. He opened his heart and let it fill him and return to her. "Certain things are meant to be, Skye. I was meant to be on that road today. Not anybody else but me. You were meant for me, nobody else, but you."

He let that settle into her a minute before tilting her head back up. "Maybe I'm the one that forced it, and you got caught in the longing of my heart." He held her gaze. "I know one thing – you hold a place in my heart." He waited a beat. "I love you. Do you love me?"

There was no waiting as her answer slipped out. "Yes, I love you."

"Good." He dipped his head and kissed her, drawing out the response she was eager to give. For a second, there was no danger, no storm, just them alone in the universe. When their lips parted, it was for her to lean weakly against him again as they stared out at the rain cascading down.

"We better get some rest," Zac said after a minute. "I have a feeling we're going to face another long day tomorrow." He drew her back to where he'd made the bed for her. This time, instead of leaving some distance between them, he settled down beside her. Tucking her into his side, he drew the blanket over them, using his body heat to help keep the chill in the air at bay.

Immediately, she sighed into him. Seemingly not at all nervous at being held by him.

"Do you think it will rain all day tomorrow?"

He almost missed her question, concentrating on the feel of her hand lying on his chest over his heart. "I'm not sure. Tropical storms are hard to predict. I didn't think this one would reach this far in, but it's dropping a lot of water. I'm thinking we've already had a couple inches. The question is, is it about done or will it stall out above us?"

He felt her breathe in deep. "Zac."

"Yes?"

"I'm really glad you're here."

"Me, too." He pressed his lips against the top of her head. "Go to sleep. I'll be here when you wake."

CR&

Skye came awake to the gentle patter of rain. The ground she lay on was hard, but she felt contentment like she'd never experienced. The hand that made little circles on her arm was soothing as was the scent that filled her senses.

Zac. She opened her eyes but his image didn't fade as it did when she came out of a viewing. Her gaze slid over the olive-colored T-shirt, over a thick neck with a prominent Adam's apple, to a strong chin shadowed by a covering of whiskers. He was really there, as was she. Above them, hard stone sheltered them from the storm just as he had sheltered her from the danger that had taken over her life.

In two days, her life had turned topsy-turvy, but feeling the man beside her, she couldn't regret any of it besides the fact he was in danger because of her. Skye barely had to shift to brush a kiss against his chest.

"Mmm, not a bad way to wake up." The words rumbled from him. "But you missed my mouth."

Skye looked up to finding him peering down at her. The mouth he mentioned curved up as her gaze fell on it. He tilted his head down as his arm drew her up. Skye stretched to complete the connection. She shivered at the first brush of his warm soft lips then she felt herself become lost in him as they settled more fully.

"Definitely a good way to wake up for the rest of my life."

Pleasure filled her for a moment before reality swept in. She pulled away and sat up.

"Skye?" He rose beside her.

"You could die because of me." She fought back the sob that pulled from her heart. "They were going to shoot you."

His hand wrapped around her arm turning her back toward him. "Don't think about it."

"How can I not? I finally feel something for a man, and I'm going to get him killed."

"So just what is it you're feeling?" His lips twitched in a way that almost pulled a smile from her.

"I'm serious."

He brushed his knuckles over her cheek. "I know. I just want to hear you say you love me again. I want to hear it every morning for the rest of my life."

"I don't know how you can say that so easy."

"Because I believe it's true and right. I tend to be kind of a straight-forward type a guy. I say what I think." He kissed the end of her nose. "You, on the other hand, have had to guard yourself. We're going to have to work on that, at least with me."

She let out a half laugh. "I still don't know how you can say that you love me so easily."

"I know it's true, that it's right."

Her breath caught at the sincerity in his blue eyes.

"I haven't dated in nearly two years. Not since I felt your touch on my mind and recognized it. I knew you were out there and that someday I had to find you. I hadn't consciously thought much about it, but I knew on getting out of the army, my next goal in life was to find you."

"You sure you're not regretting that about now?" She glanced out at the rain, then down at her hands, interlocking her fingers.

With a finger under her chin, he brought her back around to face him. "No regrets."

"You might want to change your mind about that." A tear slipped free to trickle down her cheek.

"Nah." He caught the drop, brushing it away. "When I take an assignment I finish it, and I'm just working out the payment plan."

"Payment plan?" A choked laugh escaped her. "How do I pay you for saving my life?"

"Well, if you go by fairytales, I believe it's customary for your first born. But, we don't know how long it would take to accomplish that, and I like the idea of you giving me ten years of your life. But, you're pretty young, so that might not be enough to be fair."

"So how long would be fair?" Her heart lightened with his teasing.

"I don't know. I think maybe fifty."

"I'd be old then." She pointed out.

"Yeah, you're right. I'd just have to keep you. What would our grandchildren say otherwise?"

"I think you missed a generation in there."

"That first born thing, remember, and any others we get around to. How many would you like?"

Full laughter broke from her. "We haven't even made love yet."

"Believe me. I'm planning to get around to that as soon as we get married." He smiled and placed a kiss on the inside of her wrist.

Her heart fluttered. "And when will that be?" Skye barely managed to get the words out, she felt so breathless.

"As soon as we can get out of here and find someone to marry us. You don't really want the big wedding thing do you?" He looked slightly worried.

"I don't know enough people to invite to a big wedding. I don't really have enough to do a small wedding."

"Hey." He rubbed his hands up and down her arms. "We'll work on filling your life with people."

"What about you?"

"I have plenty of people to share with you."

"Don't you want them at your wedding?" It dawned on her she was already talking like they were getting married.

He shrugged. "We can have a party after. Zan would have been my main person to be there, but since he got married without me, I'd say it's fair for me to get married without him."

"You really don't seem concerned that I might have instigated the bond between us with my mind."

"I'm not. What I feel for you is in my heart. It's an awareness of a part of me."

Skye melted at his words and the belief he put into them. "I love you."

"Now that's how you're supposed to greet me in the morning." He drew her up in his arms and kissed her.

"I've never been greeted like that in the morning." Skye felt dazed when he lifted his head.

"Does that mean you're going to marry me?"

"Yes," she said automatically then realized he'd just asked her to marry him. It had to be that shortest courtship ever but it also felt right. "Yes," she repeated firmer.

That rewarded her with another kiss. When he broke from her this time, he stood and took two steps back. "As much as I like kissing you, and believe me, I do like kissing you, I think we better get something to eat."

He turned to his pack and dug out a couple more MREs. "You're in luck. It looks like we get a cheese and vegetable omelet. It's not too bad."

Skye looked out at the rain while she ate. "Do you think we can get out of here today?"

He followed her gaze, looking up at the sky. "We'd be better off waiting for it to stop raining. We don't know what's coming in the storm and here we have protection."

"But, they know where we are."

"They know where we were. There's every possibility that they think we've moved on. They probably don't know about the overhang."

"But, they're going to be hunting me."

"The weather will hamper their efforts."

Skye noticed that he didn't try to deny the fact. "You don't think we can hide out here until after they miss the time they're to hand me over."

"That's three days. I can't see the storm lasting that long. Odds are it will blow over sometime later today."

"I want to believe this can't be happening, but all my life I've been doing what people say can't be done." The urge to scream boiled within her. It wasn't fair. She tried to never hurt anyone. She focused her life on trying to help, to make a difference, and because of that effort, she and the only person she had left in the world were in danger.

A shiver raced over her. Everyone she was ever close

to died.

"Skye?"

She looked up to find Zac watching her.

"What are you thinking?" His brows tightened.

"Nothing." As soon as she said it, she knew it wasn't completely true. If it came down to it, she'd sacrifice herself to keep him safe. She was not going to let him die around her.

He eyed her for a moment, clearly debating the truthfulness in her words.

"I was thinking, since we're not leaving, that maybe I could try to peek in on Sterling and Coons."

"Can you?"

"If they're in their office, I can locate that easily. If they're some place out, it will be a great deal more difficult, maybe impossible, but it's worth a try."

He contemplated for a moment. "Good idea. What do you need?"

"Nothing but to lay back." Skye settled on the blanket, her heart pounding. She kept her eyes focused at the back wall to reduce the chance of catching any sign of revulsion that might steal across Zac's face. He knew what she did, seemed to accept it, but seeing and knowing she was doing it might be a whole other thing. She walked outside her body, saying it that way did sound creepy.

Forcing the thought from her mind, she laid back and willed herself to relax. Closing her eyes, she drew in a deep breath and caught a faint musky smell. An image came to her mind immediately, but it was the strong features of the man who stood watch a few feet away, a man who said he loved her. Could it be true? She prayed she hadn't forced it.

"I haven't dated a woman in two years." The words echoed in her head. Her heart pounded. Skye understood the commitment behind the statement and didn't doubt it.

She wondered what he'd say if she said she'd never awakened beside a man before, then again, he'd probably already figured that out. She didn't even know much about kissing. But, she was learning fast. Warmth rushed through her.

Skye steadied her heart beat, pushed the runaway thoughts down and tried to focus on the installation. A quiver of terror stabbed through her, but she forced it away. Breathing deeply, slowing her pulse, she focused on the outer room that she'd been in only twenty-four hours earlier.

She was there by the secretary's desk. Nothing had changed.

The feeling of déjà vu hit hard. The last time she'd done this, she found they were going to sell her. What more could she find out? Steeling herself, she walked down the hall, noticing a change. The colonel's door stood wide open, something she didn't think she'd ever seen. Another wave of trepidation rolled over her, making her hesitate. Forcing herself on, she stepped in.

Sterling knelt behind his desk, his back to her. Skye moved across the room to peer over his shoulder. She looked down into a safe she didn't even know was there. Sterling pulled out several files and shoved them into a duffle bag with several others and stacks of money.

Skye gasped.

Sterling jerked and spun around. For a moment, Skye thought maybe he'd heard her, but he looked through her to the door. She turned. Wesley stood there, looking more disheveled than usual. Panic oozed from him.

Skye pulled back as Sterling closed the bag and pushed it under his desk before rising. He cut Wesley off before he could get very far into the room. "What are you doing here?" It wasn't hard to read Sterling's lips or his annoyance.

Wesley, on the other hand, spoke too fast for her to follow.

Skye figured out what he said, much of it from his

body language, as he moved from side to side. He'd been spooked by the events and wondered what they were going to do.

"Get out of here." Sterling snapped.

"But–" Wesley's objection was as clear as his fear.

Sterling said something more she didn't catch but it sent Wesley fleeing.

The colonel didn't wait. He turned back to the safe and emptied the rest of its contents.

Skye watched a moment more, then shifted across the hall to Coons' office. Though there'd never been much in the way of personal items in the room, it was now completely void of everything.

She wanted to believe it meant he'd packed up and gone, but she just couldn't accept it. Coons was one of those 'dog with a bone' mentalities. She needed to warn Zac. Skye froze. Dog – dogs. She shifted locations once more. Across the compound, behind the house Coons claimed for himself, to the kennels. The metal gate stood wide open, the pen empty. She turned to survey the area. Coons' truck was gone.

♋✇

Heart pounding, Skye opened her eyes. Her gaze went automatically to Zac. Once more, he stood as a sentinel just under the edge of the overhead stone slab, staring out into the rain. Relief filled her.

As if sensing her, he turned. His eyes ran over her then locked on her face. Silently, he crossed and knelt beside her as she sat up.

He held out a candy bar. "I thought you might need this."

Warmth spread through her. "Yes, thank you."

Her fingers brushed his palm as she took it and energy surged through her whole body. She gasped and jerked her gaze up to meet his.

Awareness blazed in his eyes. They held her then

134

lowered to her mouth. She followed the attention landing on his lips. The urge to trace her finger over them hit so strong she couldn't keep her fingers back.

His lips parted just before she made contact. The skin was surprisingly soft. She shuddered when the flesh closed down around her fingertip in a cross between a kiss and a suck.

She gasped and his lips twitched.

His hand slid back into her hair, igniting a string of fire across her senses. She watched, mesmerized, as his head dipped closer. His lips brushed her fingers again before easing past them to meet her lips. She cupped his chin as he laid claim to her mouth. She followed him in each move. The taste and feel of him familiar and right.

She floated. For a moment, she wondered if she'd left her body. Pleasure filled her, and she wondered if he could be real, or if it all wasn't just a dream. The whiskers on his chin intrigued her. He groaned when she ran her fingers over the skin, then, abruptly, he caught her wrist and pulled her hands from his face.

Like a man that had run ten miles, he drew air into his lungs.

"You can't do that." He released her, stood and walked away, putting his back to her.

"Zac." Skye stood, uncertain what she could've done wrong. Tentatively, she took a step toward him.

His back went rigid as she reached for him. She froze. Her hand hovered over the muscle, a second before she lowered it to his back. His head tipped forward.

"I can't help but kiss you." The words sounded like they'd been drug out over gravel.

Elation filled her. Skye didn't think she would ever have a man say anything like that to her. "Is that a bad thing?"

"I have to keep you safe."

"I'm afraid you lost me on that. What does one have to

do with the other?"

"When I touch you all I can think about is you." He kept his focus straight ahead. "I've waited for you for so long."

"I can't believe you mean that."

After a second, he looked back over his shoulder. "I do. You have to know, I've lived a life … it has not always been…"

She ran her hand up and down. "You have done some hard things." She understood what he was saying.

"To put it mildly."

"Yes."

He raised his hands and looked at them. "That doesn't frighten you?"

"No." This time she touched his cheek, cupping it and drawing his face around to her. "I know what kind of a man you are. The only thing that worries me, is I finally found the man I love, and I'm afraid I'm going to get him killed."

His hand covered hers. Turning his head, he pressed a kiss into her palm. "I don't plan on letting that happen. I want a lot of years with you."

"You sure?" She felt lighter than she ever had.

"I'm sure. Besides, you owe me fifty years for saving your life. It's going to take that much time just to get used to kissing you. You blow my boots off lady."

"I find that hard to believe."

"Believe it."

"I told you, I don't have much experience." She blushed.

"It's not experience. Or maybe it is – knowing you've been saving your kisses for me."

He dipped his head and kissed her hard and fast, breaking the contact before she could get lost in it. He still left her breathless. "You going to tell me what you saw?"

Reality hit her like a cold deluge.

"Sterling was clearing out his office. Wesley came in. I

couldn't make out all Sterling said but it sent him fleeing." Her throat tightened. "It looked like Coons had already cleaned out his."

He stiffened again. "The dogs?"

"I checked. They're gone."

Zac's gaze turned to outside their little sanctuary. The rain had eased, but the wind still whipped the trees. "He's already after us."

"You don't think he took off?" She couldn't help but hope.

"No. From what you said, it's not in his makeup. We need to get moving. He'll have a topographical map and all other Intel on the area. Eat that." He motioned to the candy bar she'd left on the blanket when she stood.

Skye glanced at it, she'd totally forgotten the need for fuel. Picking up the candy bar she opened it and took a bite while he stuffed things back in their pack.

"Here put this on." He handed her her jacket.

"What about you?"

"I'll be fine."

"I forgot − hard, tough ranger. Rain will bounce off you like bullets."

He grinned. "That's right. Ready to move?"

"Ready."

"We're going to move fast. Stay close and tell me if you need a break." He stressed the last.

They were soaked from pushing their way through the brush and undergrowth within the first twenty feet. What had been the small stream they leapt over the night before had doubled its size and swelled larger as they went.

Zac kept them at a constant pace. The wind picked up as they climbed out of the little gully. He was impressed that Skye didn't once complain, not even when she slipped and went down in the mud.

"You asked for it." She just grinned saucily at the mud she left on the hand he extended to help her up. After an hour, he called for a break.

"Drink."

She obeyed, downing a third of her bottle. "How long until we make it out?"

"No idea. I wish I had a map, but I'm just going on instinct. We've got to keep moving."

"One thing," she tried for optimism. "If we don't know where we're at, it stands to reason Coons doesn't either."

"If we don't accidently run into him. We don't know which way he'll be coming. He has the advantage of maps and the dogs. He'll head toward where he knows we were to pick up our trail. Our best bet is to out distance him."

"Then we better get moving." She stood.

"I want you to get plenty of rest."

"I'm fine. I'll be more careful today."

"As will I," he said firmly.

She was his to protect, and he made sure she knew it. He didn't like the not knowing where danger lay, but could work with it. He'd been trained to handle circumstances as they arose.

One thing he did know, Coons and Sterling were not going to give up until they got Skye. It wasn't just the nine million they were getting for her, which was a powerful motivation. It was what the men they made the deal with would do if they didn't deliver. He decided to keep that fact to himself.

CS80

Skye sank to the ground in relief when they stopped for lunch. Instead of one of his MREs, which she decided were pretty wonderful, they delved into things from her pack in case they had to spend another night in the woods.

She didn't mind the hiking, but she was getting tired of being wet. Her jeans stuck to her legs, and though it wasn't terribly cold, she could feel her energy being sapped.

"My plan is to keep us heading west. If my memory serves me right, we have a few more towns that way."

"And when we get there?"

"I make a couple phone calls. We get some help and report Sterling and Coons of attempted kidnapping and attempted murder. We can probably even tack on human trafficking."

"You make it sound easy."

"Once we get out, it should be."

"Let's go then." She stood, ignoring the protest of her muscles.

"Sure you're ready?"

"I want to be out of here and into dry clothes."

He smiled.

"What?"

She tipped her head to the side to study him.

"Just happy to know there's a complaint in you somewhere. I was beginning to believe you were a perfect woman. That's a daunting prospect."

"Perfect. Me? I told you people think I'm spooky."

"I've met spooky and downright scary. Trust me, you're neither." His eyes burned.

She didn't know how he did it, but in just a look, he made her feel like a beautiful, rare, intriguing woman. It flustered her and felt great.

The wind picked up again in the late afternoon. Trees creaked around them. Their bouts of conversation had come to a halt as they put all their efforts into just putting one foot in front of the other. At least for Skye, it was all she could manage. For Zac, he concentrated on detecting any sign of what might be Coons or his dogs, difficult with all the sounds the wind whipped up around them.

Skye struggled to follow him up a moss covered embankment. If it weren't for the weather and danger they faced, she would've enjoyed the hike. The area was lush and green. Blossoms covered the forest floor, blown free from the trees. It looked like a fairytale land with a tempest raging in it.

She studied the man in front of her. He might not be a prince, but he was definitely right out of her personal fairytale. She couldn't have imagined a more perfect man. Maybe that was because from the first moment she saw him, he'd held that distinction in her heart.

His hand appeared in front of her face. She caught it and let him pull her up the last little bit of the rise.

"You okay?"

"Tired," she said truthfully.

He looked around. "We can take a break over there." He pointed to a spot about twenty feet away. "It looks like it might give us some shelter." He leaned in to be heard without yelling.

Skye nodded, not sure she had the breath to answer.

He motioned for her to lead the way. They'd gone about half the distance when a gust of wind hit her, almost knocking her from her feet. Zac caught her elbow to steady her.

A sharp crack rent the air.

Her attention snapped up, just as Zac tackled her. Skye hit the ground hard with Zac coming down on top of her.

Pain jolted through her body from all points.

Zac jerked then went still, crushing her into the rich, wet earth.

It took Skye a minute to clear her mind. Branches creaked overhead ripping through the eerie stillness. She fought to take in air, and tried to shift, but couldn't. Zac was a dead weight on her.

"Zac."

He didn't answer.

Chapter Eleven

Fear stabbed into Skye. "Zac!" Had he been shot? She tried to move, but she was trapped, face down. Pressing up, she could just clear the ground enough to see over her shoulder to the crown of Zac's head. Digging her hands into the ground, she managed to drag herself forward a couple inches. She pushed up and, this time, gained enough to see more.

A large portion of a tree covered them, pinning Zac to her. Not shot. Relief left her weak then spiked again when she noticed a patch of blood dampening his hair on the side of his head.

"Zac!"

He didn't stir and she could barely get her arm back to touch him, but that didn't do any good. How bad was he hurt? He was unconscious, but what else? She tried to push up. The combined weight of the limb and Zac were too much. She gave up and slumped back down. Drawing in air as she tried to think. Stretching forward, she searched for a handhold, anything to pull herself free.

There was a large rock laid buried just out of her reach. She was glad they hadn't come down on it. Digging her fingers into the rain-soaked ground, she strained to haul herself forward. Gasping with pain and effort, she reached out and caught the stone. Her hand slipped off at her first attempt. Skye lowered her head and sucked in air, then reached again, grabbing the rock, pulling herself forward.

Her muscles screamed from the strain before she got part of her upper body free. She tried to wiggle out, but pain speared through her body. She ignored it and fought on. The stillness of him terrified her. Doubling her efforts, she clawed her way forward then froze at the sound of a groan.

"Zac!"

He stirred and groaned again. "Skye?" His voice sounded muffled.

"Are you all right?" *Stupid question. Of course he wasn't all right. He'd been unconscious.*

"What?" He broke off.

"A limb fell. You were knocked out and I can't move."

"Can't move?" That brought a sharper reaction from him.

"Trapped," she corrected quickly. "I'm not hurt. You knocked me out of the way."

His hands came to rest on the ground on either side of her, and he pressed up.

"Careful," she warned, not that it did any good.

He grunted and pushed higher, lifting himself and the branch. As soon as she was cleared, Skye shimmied out, turned and helped shove the limb to the side. He sagged back to the ground.

She crawled to him. "Let me see." She caught his hand as it went to the back of his head.

"I'm okay."

"You have a cut and you were unconscious."

"How long?"

"Not long but long enough to scare me." She studied his scalp through his hair. "It's oozing blood, and there's swelling around the area, but honestly, it doesn't look too bad."

"I'm okay." Once more he pressed on the ground and forced himself up to a kneeling position. He swayed a bit.

She caught his arm. "Zac."

His fingers locked around hers, bringing them to his lips. He kissed them.

"Those are dirty."

"So is your face." The smile he gave her was forced and ended in more of a grimace.

"You probably have a concussion."

"It wouldn't be the first, and if I do, it's not bad. No dizziness, nausea or double vision."

She studied him, wanting to believe. "What should I do?"

"Kiss me better." He managed a grin, but she could swear she still saw hints of pain in his eyes.

She leaned forward and brushed her mouth lightly over his. "Thank you."

"The best reward a man could ask for."

Before she could respond, he climbed to his feet. Skye caught a couple signs of discomfort, but he made it okay. She went to follow his action but didn't do so well. The moment her left foot touched the ground, fire lanced up her leg, as what had felt like a dull pain in her ankle exploded in full blown agony.

She cried and fell back.

"Skye!" He dropped back beside her, his hands already running down over her leg.

She gasped in air. Tears filled her eyes. It took several breaths to get herself back in control. "My ankle." She brushed moisture from her cheek. "Left."

Zac switched positions and eased her pant leg up. With tender strokes, he examined her ankle. The pain slackened to a throb until he put a little pressure on it.

Skye bit her lip to keep from crying out.

"Good thing is. I don't think it's broken, but it's definitely sprained." He pulled his pack off and dug out a bag with a large red cross on it. He removed a wrap then, laying her leg across his thighs, went to work on wrapping her ankle. His large hand moved with quick, gentle dexterity.

"You're not going to be able to walk on it. We'll slow our pace down, and you're going to have to lean on me."

"I'm sorry." She looked up, embarrassed as tears filled her eyes.

"It's not your fault." He looked up, grim faced. "I hit you."

"Yes, to save me from the tree, getting clobbered and making me a bigger hindrance than before.

He pursed his lips. "True. I think you just added ten years on to your sentence."

"Ten." A chuckle started to rise in her.

"Okay, five years and your second child." He lowered his gaze back to her ankle, running his hand over it and squeezing lightly until satisfied. "Let's try to get you on your feet." He stood and helped her up with him.

"Don't try to put any weight on it. I just want to know if you can handle having it hanging down."

"How can we—"

"We'll make it. I'm not leaving you behind. Don't even go there," he said as the thought started into her mind.

"I wasn't. I just thought that maybe I could walk a little on it."

He was already shaking his head. "I'm not risking permanent damage. I'll carry you if I need to."

"You can't. Your head." Concern blossomed in her.

"Might pound but won't fall off." He reached down in the first aid kit again, he pulled out a small bottle and dumped out a handful of tablets. "Take four. They'll help with the pain and swelling. He did likewise and took a large drink of his water bottle before handing it to her to finish.

He had the pack back on his shoulders by the time she drained it. "I guess that was our break." He slipped his arm around her waist, taking her weight on him. "We're quite a pair." He smiled down.

The pace he started them out on would have lost to a

tortoise, but as they went, they picked up speed, developing a rhythm. Skye learned fast not to put her foot down after a couple careless movements almost sent her to her knees and cost them time while she caught her breath.

ଓଃ

An hour and a half later the shadow of evening started to fill the woods. They struggled on, though. The wind had eased and rain had finally stopped completely but big drops continued to drip from the trees so that it was hard to tell.

Zac lifted Skye over a log. Her fingers trembled slightly as they gripped his arms to steady herself. Once more, she had about met her limits. He wasn't fairing much better. Luckily, the throb in his head stayed at a manageable level. Skye was right. He probably did have a concussion. Not that he could do much about it. Still he'd reached the point he needed rest as much as Skye did.

"We're going to have to find another place for the night. We're not going to make it out." He stopped and scanned the area.

"What about over there?" She pointed to a grove of trees.

"Too open. I'd rather have someplace that offers more protection. I'm afraid I may crash tonight.

Her hand tightened on his arm. "Are you all right?"

"I'm fine. Just need to get some sleep. Didn't get much the past couple nights. This beautiful woman walked into my dreams a couple nights ago and has been affecting me since."

"Beautiful?" she look skeptical.

"Oh yeah. Gorgeous."

"You really did hit your head hard."

He stepped around her so fast she fell against him. He caught her chin tipping her head up. "Gorgeous," he said firmly. The fierceness in him spoke of truth behind the words. Color flared in Skye's cheeks so deep even the low light couldn't hide it. He wanted to kiss her – to spend the rest of his life convincing her how beautiful she was.

Unfortunately, now wasn't the time. He had other priorities. Still he kissed her once hard before raising his head to look around. "Let's find some shelter."

০৪৪০

Skye nodded unable to get anything else passed the catch in her throat. Zac Masters thought she was beautiful. Gorgeous, the word echoed in her mind. Not spooky, freaky, nor any of the titles that were always associated with her.

They staggered together for a couple hundred feet more when Zac pointed out a deep impression in the side of the hill. It wasn't near as big or sheltered as the night before but it was better than anything they'd seen in the last hour.

"That way." He helped her over a rock, catching her when she almost fell. He left her clinging to a tree, while he went to check it out.

She watched as he pulled several branches out and cleared out a pile of debris. Her breath caught at the sight of something long and thin toward the back, then she went weak when she realized it was a branch, not a snake.

০৪৪০

It was actually better than he'd first thought. Zac checked the area to make sure they weren't settling into a pit of vipers –literally. To his relief, it was clear and mostly dry. The overhang had been created by a couple downed trees that crisscrossed each other, then years of dirt and leaves filled in to make a natural mortar keeping out the elements. They'd be tight, but it would work.

He had to rest. He could feel his strength slipping. He couldn't afford any error in decision. Not with Skye's life depending on him. He looked back at her. She looked worn. Her golden hair was plastered to her head and ran in tangled streams down her back. Her eyes were closed. He wondered if she was asleep against the tree.

She was utterly amazing. He knew few women who could've handled their circumstances any better than she had. Her ankle had to be killing her. He almost made it back to her when her eyes opened. She wobbled.

He reached for her. "Careful." He caught her around the waist, pulling her against him. He felt her tremble and knew it was exhaustion more than his nearness. "This will do for the night."

It seemed all she could do to nod. She started to step, obviously forgetting about her ankle. He caught her before she could place her foot down and swung her up in his arms.

Her gasp didn't hold any protest, not that it would have mattered. He crossed the short distance and knelt down, easing her to the ground.

"Thank you," she breathed out.

"You're welcome. Here." He helped slide her backpack off before removing his. "We just won't be able to have a fire tonight." He didn't say he wouldn't have risked one anyway not knowing if Coons was in the area. "I'm afraid that means we'll end up spending the night in damp clothes.

"It's okay. I'm so tired and have been waterlogged for so long, it wouldn't matter."

"Just lay back and rest while I get some water then I'll check your ankle and we can eat."

It only took him a minute to siphon water and soak a bandana. He returned to find her curled in a ball, asleep. He pulled the blanket from her pack and draped it over her. He wished they could have gotten out of the wet clothes. Fortunately, the air wasn't chilled enough to warrant it.

He rubbed his hands over his face, glancing over his shoulder at the approaching night. They'd made it another day. It was less than twenty-four hours to the deadline Skye mentioned when they were to turn her over. The question was, could they avoid them that long with Coons and his dogs hunting them and Skye's injured ankle.

He ran his fingers back through his hair, gently touching the bump. He had a headache and a concussion. Not good. He had to have rest. He could feel his mind shutting down. Opening the pill container, he shook a couple into his hand and swallowed them down with some water. Rest could come in a few minutes. First, Skye needed food. They both did. They'd burned a lot of calories today. Luckily, one thing MREs were good for was restoring calories.

He prepped the food. Skye didn't even stir. He decided to let her sleep while he consumed his then shifted their packs around. It didn't take long to have them settled for the night and he turned his attention back to her. He needed to check her ankle.

⋐⋛⋩

Skye came awake to twinges of pain in her ankle, but the gentle stroking of large hands on the swollen flesh made up for the discomfort. She jerked a little at the cold cloth draped over the sensitive flesh then sighed as relief eased in.

"Sorry." Zac's voice rumbled over her like a caress.

"It's okay. I fell asleep again."

"You were exhausted. You're going to think I'm an impossible taskmaster."

"You mean you're not?" The tease rose in her bringing up her mood.

"Probably." His lips pulled up in a smile she could barely make out in the low light.

"But you're harder on yourself than anyone else." A fact not a question. Zac would run himself into the ground to see to what he saw as his responsibility. "Have you had any rest?"

Ignoring her question, he said, "I ate without you." He handed her the food packet. It was still warm. "Eat."

She obeyed, taking a few bites. She suddenly felt

ravenous and no food had ever tasted better.

He watched her a minute then turned his attention away. Ever the watchdog, but her guard looked a little gray around the gills, not that he'd ever admit to it. She took another bite. "You're a good cook."

He turned back and laughed.

That was better. "Are you going to get some rest now? I can stay up and watch." As exhausted as she was, she was even more worried about Zac. He needed rest. She was certain he had a concussion. The last hour before they'd stopped she could see the tightening around his eyes and an occasional misstep that spoke of pain. He'd also grown quiet, stoic.

She thought for a moment he hadn't heard her, then he blinked. "That's not necessary. I was just waiting until dark." He shifted to sit beside her and leaned his head back against the dirt wall. "Finish eating and we'll get some sleep. If anyone comes close, I'll wake." His words grew softer.

Skye didn't doubt him. She quickly finished eating, surprised she managed to down most of it.

The moment she started to close it, Zac opened his eyes, his focus going right to the meal pack. "Good."

He sounded satisfied, then reached over and picked up the biscuit she'd left. He ate it while she disposed of the rest like she'd seen him do. When she finished she turned back to find him holding out a small candy bar, from the stash in her backpack.

"Want to share?" he asked, his voice low and tempting.

"There was dessert." She pointed out. "I just ate mine."

"Yes, but this is chocolate." He wiggled it back and forth.

Unable to resist, she snatched it from him and tore open the wrapper, taking a bite before holding the rest out to him. Instead of taking it, he leaned forward and closed his mouth over the offered piece, eating it from her hand.

The warmth in his eyes wrapped around her. His gaze dropped to her mouth.

The chocolate melted there becoming richer and more decadent than it ever had been.

"You know the first time I kissed you, I could swear I tasted a touch of chocolate." His voice was as silky as the taste in her mouth. He cupped her cheek, tipping her head to him as he lowered his mouth. Skye opened, allowing him access. He settled gently and slipped in. The taste of him mingled through the chocolate to become the most alluring thing she had ever tasted.

She sighed as his head lifted.

"Sleep well, Skye."

She looked up to find his eyes studying her. He then settled back, crossing his arms over his chest. His breathing slowed immediately. She couldn't believe he was actually asleep that fast. Still, he had to be as tired as she was. Concern hit her. His concussion. Should she be worried about it? Was it safe for him to be asleep, at least deeply asleep? Did she need to wake him every hour?

She didn't know much about first aid, never needed to, but when she got out of here, she was going to learn. What ifs started to come to her mind but she forced them back before fear could blossom. She had faith in Zac.

The shadows had lengthened to the point she could hardly make him out, still her heart caught. She'd learned so much about him the last two days, and it hadn't changed anything she already knew or felt before, except maybe strengthening her feelings. He was an honorable man. A good man. She respected him, but her feelings went deeper. She really did love him and it wasn't just there, in the back of her imagination. It was buried in her heart

She settled back to be close to him, careful not to disturb his sleep. She studied the outline she could barely make out of his face. He had a great chin, strong, made more prominent when he set it but now, even relaxed, it was still tough. Stubble covered it, giving him the tough guy look that was so popular on TV or in the movies right now. It was a good look for him but she knew instinctively that as soon as he got back to civilization, the hint of a beard would come off. Zac might be the tough macho type guy, but he was also the clean shaven type.

A twinge of concern of a different type hit her. He liked control and organization. He was used to it from the military and engineering, but he was talking of hooking himself together with a woman who walked outside of her body and wanted to make jewelry and crafts for a living. Could they be more opposite?

But he felt so right. If he would have her, she would have him. Life was so crazy with everything that was happening. One thing held her together. She loved him.

Tentatively, she reached out and laid a finger on his chest, over his heart. Just to make sure he was breathing fine, she told herself. Skye let the strong heartbeat calm her and closed her eyes then opened them again when his hand settled over hers, pressing her palm down. His other arm came around her and pulled her into him, so her head was cradled against his shoulder.

"Sleep."

The single word carried love in it and was followed up by the feel of his lips brushing her temple as he leaned his head against hers. Skye closed her eyes and slept, knowing that was where she wanted to be the rest of her life.

⋘⋙

The next day was continuing much like the previous, but Zac was getting concerned. They were low on rations after finishing off their last MRE for breakfast. He also wanted to get Skye's ankle x-rayed, though he was convinced it was just sprained, he wanted to be sure. Even soaking it in the cool water of a stream every time they stopped to rest hadn't done much to bring down the swelling.

They had two things in their favor, now. After the rest he'd gotten, he felt back to normal with only a slight headache that morning that faded as the day went on. They only had to avoid Coons and Sterling for a few hours more and the men would miss their deadline to hand her over.

Again, he thought of tucking them away somewhere and just waiting them out. He and Skye would have another night in the woods, which they could handle easily enough, even without food. The problem was he had no doubt Coons and his dogs were still after them and every minute they'd be getting closer.

He stared at the ridge behind them. He could swear he could feel them getting closer.

"Time to go." He turned and crossed the few feet back to Skye. Reaching her as she lifted her ankle out of the water, he dried it with his spare T-shirt and went to work rewrapping it. There was no getting her shoe on. Not that it mattered, because she couldn't put any weight on it.

She hissed in a breath of pain, but didn't say anything. He looked into her eyes.

"I'm okay."

He didn't know how many times she'd assured him of that. "You're much more than okay." He rose up on his knees to kiss her. He loved to kiss her and the way she reacted. Love, all for him.

"Come on." He helped her up, before handing her the branch he'd fashioned for a crutch and wrapping his arm around her. She didn't bemoan about slowing them down, which he appreciated. She just went on the best she could.

It was a slow process climbing the hill. Skye leaned into him, trying to catch her breath as he surveyed their surroundings. The trees were so thick it was hard to pick out anything, but he could swear he could make out a break into the foliage then he saw a flash of red metal, a car.

"There's a road."

Skye jerked at his words then slumped against him.

"Finally." The elation that poured from her was cut off by the low bay of a hound in the distance. Her eyes went from searching for the road to him. Fear radiated in them, washing away her seconds of relief.

As one, they moved forward down the slope in a well-rehearsed motion. Zac kept them going as fast as he dared, conscious of Skye's ankle. She hissed out a burst of pain when she slipped slightly, touched her ankle down.

Zac held in the curse he felt rising in him. He couldn't take her pain any longer. He stopped, pulled off his pack with her belongings now stuffed inside.

"Put this on." She didn't argue. He helped her fasten the strap across her chest, then turned his back to her. "On." Again she didn't hesitate wrapping her arms around his neck and her legs around his waist as he stood.

Zac started down the hill the instant she was settled. Fortunately, the slope wasn't steep. They covered the ground at a fast pace.

"The last person who gave me a piggy back ride was my father and I was a little girl."

"This one might be a hair rougher," he ground out, focusing on where he placed his feet.

They made it to the bottom of the slope but instead of releasing her, he continued on increasing their speed, covering the ground quickly with his long, loping stride. He knew they had to be getting close to the road. Then he heard a vehicle just ahead.

"Hang on." He quickened his pace, pushing through the brush. Bushes tore at them. Skye clung to him, her arms low on his chest so she didn't choke him. They burst through onto the road in time to see a white vehicle, with a black push bumper on front and a light bar top.

"It's a sheriff's vehicle," Skye cried out. Her relief as strong as his.

She started to wave one hand over her head as he made it to the edge of the road.

The car pulled to a stop as Zac lowered her to the ground. She hugged him. Exaltation bubbled from her. For a split second, he shifted his attention from the car to Skye.

"Put your hands up and back away from the woman."

Chapter Twelve

Zac looked up.

The sheriff stood by his car, gun pointed directly at him. The man's muscles were set tight, stating the degree of intent behind the words.

Zac didn't know what he'd been told, but whatever it was, the man was prepared to shoot.

Zac lifted his hands slowly above his head, conscious of the fact Skye needed him for balance.

"What? No." She turned toward the Sheriff, placing herself between them.

"Move away from him. It's all right," the sheriff assured her. He was older, with a slight paunch over his belt, but he also appeared to be shrewd.

"Please, we need help," Skye implored.

"I said, move away," the sheriff said sharply. The muscles tightened around his eyes.

"Skye, do it," Zac said softly.

The sheriff was looking between them. "Quiet!" he snapped. "No talking."

"She hurt her ankle and can't step on it." Zac kept his voice calm. "Can I help lower her to the ground?"

The sheriff glanced at her ankle. The wrap was plain to see, as was the way she held her foot up, and hopefully the lawman had seen him carrying her.

Zac read the debate on his face and knew the moment he made his decision.

The sheriff nodded. "Take off the backpack first. Real slow with one hand at a time. Keep the other so I can see it at all times, and toss it to the side.

Zac complied and tossed the pack a good six feet from them before returning his hands to above his head.

"All right, again with one hand lower her to the ground. Keep the other hand up." The tip of his gun made a slight motion to the sky.

Zac took her hands, locking his muscles, and lowered her like he was doing curls with weights. The moment she settled on the ground, the next command came.

"Hand up. Move away. Now! On your knees and cross your ankles."

Zac took three steps forward, keeping his body as much as he dared between Skye and the sheriff but to the side enough that the man could still see her and not get any antsier than he was.

The sheriff came forward his attention going between them. Obviously confused about what he was finding and what he'd been told.

"Please, what are you doing?" Skye tried again as the sheriff slipped a pair of plastic restraints on Zac's wrists. "We need help. We haven't done anything wrong."

The man ignored her, patting him down and removing his pocketknife. He stepped back, eying her. "I guess you won't be going anywhere. Still, neither of you move." The sheriff walked backward to his car and pulled out his phone, using it instead of the mic on his uniform.

"Colonel, your daughter has been found."

"No!" Skye cried out.

He ignored her and added a location then hung up. Looking over at Skye, he shook his head. "Girl, you've caused a whole lot of trouble. If I was you, I'd just keep my mouth shut until your father gets here. It won't be long."

"He's not my father."

The sheriff wasn't listening to her and when Skye

scooted forward, he put his gun away and pulled his Taser from his belt.

"Skye!" Zac knew he had to get the guy's attention, and the sound of a hound rippling down the hill upped the need to hurry. "Listen, arrest us. Take us to jail. Just do it before Sterling gets here. He tried to kill me and kidnap her. She isn't his daughter. She worked at the government installation. They want information she has."

The dogs howled again, a lot closer than they'd seemed before. Zac glanced at the woods then back. "Those are dogs. They're after her. They've been hunting her. Would a father send dogs out after his daughter?" He could see the man thinking, wavering. "Take us to jail. Lock us up. Just don't let them get hold of her."

"Please." Skye pleaded. "Look at me. I'm old enough that even if he was my father, I can make my own choices. Zac didn't kidnap me. He saved me when they tried to – No!" She ended on a cry as a familiar, big, black truck came around the curve.

The sheriff glanced back. "We'll get this all sorted out, now."

Even before Coons' truck reached them, Zac could tell Coons wasn't driving but the stark-white hair told him exactly who was. "Get her in your car now. She's not safe." This time he made it his giving orders voice.

The sheriff jerked and automatically stepped forward. He was half-way to Skye before he faltered. "There's no concern. You just stay put." He focused on Zac.

Before anymore could be said, the truck pulled to a stop.

Sterling stepped out with a genial smile plastered on his face. "Skye, sweetie."

False relief poured from the Colonel, then again, maybe it wasn't false. If he didn't hand her over, he'd be in a bad situation.

"Sheriff. You found her. How can I thank you?"

157

"You can give me some answers. I got the impression your daughter was quite a bit younger." The sheriff rested his free hand on his hip not far from his gun.

"I apologize for that. I guess I just think of her that way. And she doesn't have much experience in the world." Sterling's smile was sickly sweet and condescending.

"You're not my father!" Skye yelled and pulled back as he came toward her.

"Stop that. You wouldn't want to see anyone get hurt now would you?" Sterling's gaze went to Zac, giving Skye an obvious warning.

"What's going on here?" the sheriff demanded, clearly uneasy.

Before anyone could answer, a rustling in the trees drew everyone's attention. A second later two hounds burst out on the road. The dogs bared their teeth and focused in on Skye. Zac shifted his body so he was in between her and the dogs. The sheriff didn't comment, shifting the Taser to his other hand and pulling his gun back out.

The precaution wasn't necessary as Coons stepped from the trees. "Down!" Coons ordered. The dogs dropped, their snouts on the ground, bodies tense, ready to spring at the word.

"Good timing." Coons looked to Sterling.

"Wh–," the Sheriff's question cut off as Sterling stepped up behind him and slammed a gun butt into the side of the man's head. The sheriff dropped in an unconscious heap.

"I didn't want to have to do that." Sterling didn't look too concerned.

"Told you we didn't need to worry." Coons sneered.

"Precautions. Needed something in place if they made it to the authorities."

Coons grunted. "Let's get 'er loaded." He sauntered toward them.

Zac could hear Skye scoot back again, but he waited.

Not moving until Coons passed him, he ducked his head and rolled, coming up on his feet. Plowing into Coons, Zac took them both to the ground.

Coons reacted fast, grabbing for him, but Zac was faster. He kicked out, scissoring his legs around the man then clamped down, his thighs around Coons' neck.

The dogs charged forward snapping at Zac. He rolled, placing Coons between them. Coons twisted and squirmed, trying to break free. Zac locked his muscles, ignoring Coons' efforts to pry his leg away. He could feel the man weaken. A blow struck his back. Pain seared through his nerves. His muscles constricted and jerked as electricity coursed through his body.

He was aware of Skye yelling for him but couldn't do anything to make his overloaded system respond.

ೲ

Skye bit her lip to keep from crying out. Never would she have imagined anyone being able to do what Zac did, especially with his hands fastened behind his back. There was no way Coons could break the hold. Her attention was so wrapped in the fight, she'd forgotten about Sterling until, out of the corned of her eye, she saw him lean over the sheriff. He stood, walked toward them and extended his hand.

Skye screamed seeing the black shape he held. Instead of a sharp report of a gun, an odd hiss sounded. Something flew out and struck Zac in the back. He jerked, groaned, and went ridged. She screamed again.

Coons broke Zac's hold and rolled to the side, gasping in air several seconds before he kicked out, catching Zac in the side.

Zac didn't react to the blow, still wrapped in the effects of the Taser.

"Hold." Coons ordered the dogs and climbed to his feet. Rubbing his throat, he glared down at Zac then shifted his attention to the dogs. "Kennel." He pointed down the road in the general direction that would lead to the base.

The hounds didn't hesitate at the command. They took off at a run. Coons watched them for a second then turned, and pulled back his foot to kick Zac again.

Skye launched herself at him, falling short and crying out as her foot hit the ground, but her action was enough, along with Sterling's order to stop Coons.

"Enough! Let's go before someone calls to check on the sheriff. Nice of him to cuff our friend here." He crossed the rest of the distance between them, looked down and pursed his lips. "I was planning on leaving Lt. Colonel Masters behind, but now, I think it might be prudent to bring him with us."

"Why? Just put a bullet into him if you're worried," Coons said.

"No!" Skye flattened herself over Zac.

"And you have your reason." Sterling pointed at her with a grin. "It seems our little nest egg has formed an attachment for the Lt. Colonel. I think she will be much more cooperative if she knows her actions will not only be responsible for keeping him alive, but the condition he remains in. Isn't that right?" He turned his attention to her. "Do you understand what I'm saying? Army Rangers are noted for being able to take a lot of pain."

Skye's stomach churned. Bile rose in her throat. Once more she'd brought danger and pain to Zac. As if knowing her thoughts were on him, Zac raised his head. His jaw was still clenched and there were shadows of pain in his eyes. He didn't say anything, but rolled over so he brushed her leg with his side in a way she knew was intentional.

Skye laid her hand on his arm and let it slide down until she came in contact with the restraints. Zac brought his hand up enough to wrap his fingers around hers.

"Let's get them loaded." Sterling bent, gripping her arms, ripping away the connection with Zac and sliding a pair of plastic cuffs around her wrists. "Precautions." He met her glare. "I think I'll keep this Taser handy, in lieu of a cattle prod. I imagine The Viper can come up with one of those, or he might have his own preferable means. We might even be able to parlay Lt. Colonel Masters into a bonus. The means to get her to do what they want."

Skye's stomach clenched and she went cold. "No." Her cry escaped as a whisper.

Sterling looked down and smiled a big, wolfish grin. "Or we could always just drop him off in the gulf. Say from a thousand feet, without a parachute. Even Rangers can't survive that." His lip twitched. "The only thing left would be chum for the sharks.

There was so much pleasure in the taunt, Skye couldn't help wonder what she'd ever done to warrant that kind of venom.

"We'll put her inside and him in back. I don't want them together. They might get it in their heads to try to escape. If they're separated and one tries to escape, they'll know what their actions will mean to the other.

Coons stepped to her. Reflexively, Skye pulled back to avoid the hand reaching for her.

He sneered down. "Looks like The Spook hasn't learned her lesson yet." Coons locked on her arm.

Zac shifted so fast, he rolled into Coons legs, taking them out from under him before Coons could start to react. Coons still had hold of Skye's arm, pulling her over. She fell coming down on her shoulder. A cry burst from her, then changed to a gasp as Zac pulled up to throw himself to the ground beside her, coming down on Coons arm with his elbow and body.

The sergeant cried out.

Zac was already moving. Rolling, he made it to his feet, diving for Sterling. The colonel stumbled back, getting the Taser up to fire seconds before Zac crashed into him.

Zac's body jerked as the electricity overloaded his system for a second time. Both men went down.

For a moment, the whole forest seemed stunned into silence. Skye started to reach for Zac but caught sight of the sheriff and changed direction. She pulled, dragged herself, then finally resorted to rolling on the ground to reach the fallen lawman. Sterling had taken his gun and the Taser, but with any luck, he might have a phone in his pocket.

Skye pulled herself along, but with her hands tied her progress was slow. A cry burst out behind her. Skye glanced back. The sound wasn't from Zac. Sterling stirred, but Coons was the one pulling himself to his feet.

He swayed and brought his foot back, kicking Zac in the side. Skye flinched and continued to pull herself across the ground. She was only a few feet from the Sheriff when she heard another thud and another as Coons kicked Zac several more times.

"Halt."

Skye froze at Sterling's command but a glance back had her realizing it hadn't been issued to her. Zac lay lax on the ground.

"I just told you he was useful."

Coons swore. Agony covered his face along with his rage. "He dislocated my shoulder." The words ground out of him in pain.

"And you can be satisfied with what he's bringing by being alive. Now, let's get him in the truck."

Skye reached the sheriff and used him to pull her close enough to search for his phone, but before she could, a booted foot came down on her wrist.

"I could always break your arm." Sterling pressed down.

Skye sucked in air and rolled to look up at the man. He glared at her, still applying pressure until tears came to her eyes. The instant he moved his foot, he reached down and pulled her up.

Skye barely managed to keep her foot from touching the ground but everything swam around her and for a moment she thought she was going to faint again. Sterling must have also because he swung her over his shoulder. They were at the truck before her vision cleared. He opened the doors and dropped her in back. She lit on the edge of the seat and slipped off to the floor, not that he took notice. He shoved her legs in and slammed the door.

For a second, all Skye could do was drag the air into her lungs and let it out. Tears threatened but she pushed them back. It took some squirming around to maneuver herself onto the seat so she could see out.

Sterling, with some one-handed assistance from Coons, dragged Zac toward the truck. His eyes remained closed. Tears stung hers. All her fears came to be. They had her, but worst, they had Zac. His life was even more endangered because of her.

She lost sight of him while they went around the back until Sterling lowered the tail gate. Helplessly she watched as Zac was shoved into the back of the truck. She cringed when Coons pulled a bike cable out of a box and handed it to Sterling, who ran in through the bands fastened around Zac wrists and used a lock to fasten it to a cargo loop in the truck bed. Sterling then reached into the same box and pulled out a roll of duct tape and tore off a strip, placing it over Zac's mouth.

He looked up and met her gaze through the window. There was promise in his eyes. He flipped the roll in the air and caught it. A shiver went through her as she got the implied threat. If she said or tried anything, he'd tape her mouth too.

She jerked when Coons opened the passenger door and climbed in, collapsing back into the seat. He groaned then his eyes met hers in the rearview mirror. "Any excuse and your boyfriend," he made it sound vile, "is dead."

She pulled her gaze from him and watched silently as Sterling drove the police car up next to the sheriff, got out and used the real, old-fashioned type handcuffs to fasten the sheriff's wrists before dragging him into the backseat. He checked the door locks, then got back in, driving the car off the road into the trees.

If Skye wouldn't have known where it was, she wouldn't have noticed the vehicle, it was shrouded so completely. Sterling appeared back through the shrubbery a second later and climbed in the truck.

"He won't be calling for assistance any time soon."

"Should have just killed him," Coons mumbled.

"That's the mentality that gets you hunted no matter where you go."

"We're not coming back to the states ever again and you know it." He groaned. "I need a doctor before we go. I won't make it on a plane ride." He leaned against the door then shifted again, as if trying to get comfortable.

Skye pressed her face to the back window watching the road disappear behind them and for any sign of Zac regaining consciousness. Several miles passed before he stirred. Another minute and another mile sped by before he tugged on his tethered wrists and tried to sit up.

Fastened the way he was, he couldn't make it high enough to see over the sides of the truck-bed but his twisting allowed him to look up at her.

"Are you all right?" He mouthed the words.

She nodded.

"How long?"

Skye tried to calculate. It seemed like he'd been out an eternity but actually it wasn't that long. "Ten." She tried to mouth back. When he didn't seem to get it she repeated it, then tapped her head softly on the window ten times.

It was his turn to nod. "Hands?"

She made a motion of trying to lift them

He nodded immediately, and his head slumped back down. His eyes closed then opened. "Need rest," he said.

She knew it was to calm her when his eyes closed again. Skye followed his actions and rested her head on the seat back. Weariness gnawed at her. Her body was well past the point where it craved rest. The next thing she was aware of was the sound of a car coming up on them.

Skye raised her head. A small, silver compact gained on them. It gleamed like hope as it pulled up to overtake them. She wished her hands were free so she could wave them down, but all she could do was plead with her eyes, which really didn't convey the need over the distance, even if the occupants noticed her.

"Get down!" Sterling snapped.

When she didn't react, Coons reached over the seat with his good arm and caught her by the hair, yanking her backwards.

"He said down." He groaned but continued to pull until she slipped off the seat just before she heard the car pass.

The sound of agony that came from Coons brought her some satisfaction, but before she could savor it, Sterling pulled the truck to the edge of the road, stopped and got out.

Skye wiggled back to the seat. Fear flared as she watched him walk to the back. He pulled his gun and pointed it at Zac.

Zac's eyes opened again, but Sterling didn't meet his gaze, he raised his eyes to her. Her heart pounded off the seconds. In a smooth motion, Sterling holstered the gun then reached into the truck bed. Skye's breath caught but instead of reaching for Zac, he caught the edge of a tarp and pulled it over him, tucking it around him so she couldn't see him.

A minute later, he climbed back behind the wheel. Skye met his gaze in the rearview mirror. "Next time, I put a bullet in him. Now stay down."

She slid onto the floor, fighting back a wave of nausea as the truck lurched back on the road. A couple minutes later it slowed again. Skye craned her neck to see out but didn't risk rising. Still, she managed to catch glimpses of a few taller buildings, but none looked at all familiar to her. She wondered just how far they'd traveled while she'd been out of it, or if it was just an area she didn't know.

They wove their way through the town before they finally came to a stop.

"Go get your shoulder taken care of then call me, but be quick about it. We need to be out of here in two and a half hours to make our rendezvous with Vibora. The instant Coons closed the door, they pulled away and drove several more minutes before stopping.

Sterling turned in the seat and looked back at her. "I'm going to grab some food. The truck will be in my view at all times, so unless you want Masters to get another shock, you better not try anything." That said he got out, slamming and locking the door.

Skye sat on the floor and fought down tears, not knowing what she should do. She didn't doubt Sterling would shoot Zac. The only problem was doing what Sterling said wouldn't leave Zac any safer.

⋘⋙

The mugginess in the air was ten times worse under the tarp, but it was starting to cool. The sun must be going down. At least it gave Zac an idea how much time had passed.

The worse thing was him not being able to see Skye. He tried to reassure himself that she was still there. He felt her near and his logic backed it up.

When they first stopped only one person got out. They'd driven a couple more minutes, then the other, he figured Sterling had gotten out. Neither time had they opened the backdoor to get Skye out.

He'd started to doze when the driver returned, but they hadn't moved location. He slept further losing his lock on time, but it was long enough that his mind cleared and his body recuperated to a more functioning degree.

When the engine finally started again they went a short

distance and only stopped long enough for someone to climb in. Coons he was certain, then they started to drive again. He estimated they'd been traveling a couple hours. That fit with the cooling temperature. Zac wished he could see out to get an idea where they were.

What he really wanted was to see Skye. The last glimpse of her, her face had been pale. Not surprising with what she'd been through. They wouldn't hurt her. She was too valuable, but the knowledge didn't relieve the ache in him.

Zac worked at the tie binding his wrists, rubbing it against the rough edge he'd found on the bolt fastening him to the truck-bed. He wore a large tear in the plastic but it was still holding tight. He had to get free. If they got on the plane, he was a dead man, and he didn't want to contemplate what would happen to Skye.

The problem was, after as many rescue operations she'd helped with, there would be no one to rescue her. It wasn't hard to make someone disappear when few people knew she existed. How long had Sterling been planning this? Had he intentionally been keeping Skye from other people with this in mind or was it just to lessen her opportunity to meet, fall in love and want to leave.

He didn't doubt Sterling had instigated her self-image that she was a freak. Zac shook his head that she could believe that, but knew she'd been tagged with it all her life, so what wasn't to believe? Well, he'd spend the rest of his life convincing her how beautiful and special she was and not because of her ability.

They slowed and turned off the main road. Zac had to shift to keep his head from bumping as they went over a couple rough patches. They stopped, then after about thirty seconds pulled forward.

The meet. Time was up.

ೞ

Skye eased up as they came to a stop. When neither

Sterling nor Coons snapped at her she edged onto the seat and followed their focus out the front window. A field stretched out in front of them. A large clumping of trees set off to one side, but it was the plane, with a ramp in back lowered to the ground, that drew her attention. Two men stood at the bottom edge, guns held across their bodies.

As she watched, two more men appeared at the top of the ramp. One stood tall and shifted behind the other, obviously another guard. She studied the other man. He was medium height. The late afternoon sun gleamed off his black hair and highlighted his sharp, chiseled features. His lips twisted in a self-satisfied smile. Skye shivered. Coons and Sterling looked tame compared to this man.

Sterling got out of the truck and held his hands above his head.

The man glanced down at his watch in a movement that Skye knew was merely for show. He lifted and lowered his head in a single motion as a sign of acceptance. "You are on time. I would expect no less from a military man." His voice was a low rumble that barely slithered its way into the open door of the cab. "The Colonel, I presume."

Skye figured there was no presumption about it. He knew exactly who he was dealing with. This man, Vibora, was careful about who he met with.

"You have the merchandise?"

A shiver slithered deep in her. She was the merchandise.

"Yes." Sterling motioned back toward the truck and her.

Coons got out, his arm in a sling. He'd ranted on the drive about his dislocated shoulder and a fractured humerus. He'd wanted to kill Zac, only his glee that Zac was in for worse kept him from doing it.

Seeing the man in front of Sterling, Skye feared Coons was right. Dread coiled around her heart.

She scooted back on the seat as Coons opened the door

revealing her. Under the man's hard, black, penetrating eyes, terror stronger than any she'd felt so far struck her.

"So this is the seer." His brows tightened as his eyes lingered on her. "She is not much compared to her pictures."

Skye was thankful for every smudge of grime that covered her.

Coons reached in with his good arm, caught her tethered wrists and pulled her forward to the edge of the seat, then out. Skye barely managed to land keeping her injured foot up. She caught the wicked twist of Coons' lips. Payback for the pain and trouble he suffered, he didn't care that it was his own actions that led to it.

"She is injured," Vibora observed, disproval evident in his voice.

"Just sprained her ankle trying to get away. Nothing to affect her abilities, I assure you," Sterling placated.

Vibora's eyes tightened slightly. "Yes?"

Skye watched as he crossed his arms over his chest then flexed his fingers one by one before relaxing them. "You had some trouble and wish to add transport out of the country as part of your fee." The man's tone was icy.

"Yes," Sterling said quickly obviously reading some of the tension in the air she felt. "But, we brought you some compensation that I think you will find more than covers that." Sterling started to the back of the truck then froze as one of the guards jerked up his gun, pointing it directly at him.

"Easy." Sterling raised his hands again. "I brought you the key to her cooperation."

Vibora studied him a second then with the motion of one finger, the guard moved to Sterling.

"Open." The single word growled out in command from the guard.

Skye focused on the tarp as Sterling carefully lowered the tailgate and pulled the cover aside.

Greedily, her eyes took in the sight of Zac. Her heart dropped when he shifted. It seemed to take him a lot of effort just to raise his head an inch. His eyelids opened to about half mast, and he made no act of recognition that he saw her.

Skye missed what was said behind her, but she understand the answer that the guard returned. "A man."

"Not just any man." Smugness filled Sterling's voice. He, too, was taking pleasure in her and Zac's situation. "It is the man she loves and will do anything for." He grabbed Zac by the leg and pulled him to the end of the gate.

At the same time, Skye gripped the side of the truck and hopped to the end then dove for Zac to catch him as Sterling pulled him off the tailgate. With her injured ankle and tied hands, there was no way she could prevent Zac's dropping. Still, she tried to cushion his impact but his weight was too much for her, and they both fell. She cried out with the brief touch of her foot to the ground. Lights flashed before her eyes. Her ears rang and for a moment she thought she might pass out.

"Her key." Vibora voice cut through the haze.

"He will assure her cooperation. I hope you will agree that makes up for our passage."

Skye drew in air and lifted her head in time to see intrigue tighten Vibora's features. "Let's see this key."

Sterling reached down and hauled Zac up, tearing him away from her. She bit the inside of her cheek to keep from protesting. It tore at her when Zac staggered and sagged against the tailgate. He'd seemed so strong earlier but the Taser hits had taken a lot out of him, that or his efforts to carry her out of the woods. It was all her fault. He was in this situation because of her.

Tears welled up in her eyes. She blinked them down. She couldn't do anything that could lead to him being hurt more. The question was – what was best. Should she try to mask her feelings or let them be seen?

Before she could decide Vibora spoke. "I agree he might be of use, but first, let's finish our transaction. I would see proof of your claims. The files you provided gave intriguing possibilities, but I would see for myself."

Skye stiffened, but before she could react, strong, brown fingers wrapped around her arm and pulled her up. She didn't have to worry about her foot touching the ground as she was hoisted unceremoniously over the guard's shoulder.

"What does she need?" Vibora asked.

"A place to relax and the coordinates is all," Sterling shifted slightly. He, too, was nervous.

She barely caught Vibora's nod as the guard holding her turned. One of the other guards disappeared back inside the plane. The guard carried her to the bottom of the ramp just as the other returned with a zero gravity folding lounge chair. Skye wondered if Vibora had been anticipating the answer and quickly decided he was. As she was tipped back, the second guard caught her shoulders and helped lower her to the chair.

It was then she saw that another man had come out of the plane. He carried a glass case with a large, thick, brown snake, with what looked-like black splotches, coiled inside.

Before she could react to it, she was rocked back, pulling a gasp from her. Vibora leaned down toward her. "Are you going to cooperate, or do I have to apply the key? My friend here does not have a good disposition. You would not want to make it mad. The viper's fangs fold back but are long to penetrate deep. Its venom causes much pain, the tissue dies and sometimes the man, as it causes internal bleeding."

Though he didn't break his gaze from her, her eyes went to Zac, to the serpent in the case, and back to Zac. He still rested on the end of the truck with his head down, but she could swear there was an alertness about him.

"Your answer."

The sharp words made her jump again. She swallowed and nodded, not trusting her voice.

"The coordinates." He dropped a piece of paper in her lap. "I will know if what you say is the truth."

Chapter Thirteen

Skye stared at the numbers and tried to force herself to relax, but the case with the snake kept drawing her focus. Her heart pounded. The serpent lifted its head, black eyes glistened at her through the glass. Its tongue flicked out. She cringed remembering reading that it was linked to a snake's taste or ability to smell. It was tasting the air – tasting her fear.

"Please." As much as she didn't want to show weakness, she knew she had to. "Take the snake away. I can't ..." she broke. Feeling the weight of Vibora's gaze, she couldn't pull air into her lungs. His eyes were as black as the viper's. "I ... have to ... calm." She tried to swallow to loosen the tightness in her throat, but it didn't do any good.

Vibora nodded and the man with the snake went back into the plane.

Skye sagged back in the lounge and sucked in a breath. It froze in her lungs as Vibora pulled a knife from a sheath strapped to his leg. Light glinted off the wide, wicked looking blade as he lowered it toward her. He slipped it in between her wrists and sliced easily through the plastic cuffs blinding her hands.

Keeping her attention focused on him, she rubbed the skin chaffed from the bonds. This time, she slowly drew in a deep breath and let it out. Closing her eyes, she repeated the process several times before she could start to relax her muscles one at a time. It was only her amount of experience that allowed her to let go of what was happening around her. She opened her eyes, looked at the coordinates, then closed her eyes again and let herself drift, concentrating only on the location on the piece of paper.

One moment she was in her body, the next she was across the world, standing in a heavy foliaged forest. She turned in a circle, taking in the growth and trying to get her bearings. Tall, broad-leaf plants surrounded her, obscuring any view. She moved forward about twenty feet and found more of the same.

Making a hundred and eighty degree turn, she went back the other way. Not far from her starting point, she entered a clearing cut to make room for a long, shabbily constructed building that was really just a roof over a row of roughhewn tables. Parked at one end was an old, beat up two-ton truck that had to be from the sixties or older. Its big flatbed was sided with sagging timbers. To its side, sat a small-sized pickup that showed the signs of once being red but was now more rust and holes than anything.

Skye moved forward studying the area, not seeing a single person. She glanced up seeing the netting strung through the canopy above her. Almost to the barn, she caught sight of the of four small, weathered men in dirty, loose-fitting clothes as they came out from the trees and shuffled between tables stacked with piles of dried leaves.

Skye froze at the sight on the man that followed them. Easily twice their size, dressed in fatigues similar to the military garb of Vibora's men, he held a gun cradled across his body. He glared and ordered something that made the men scurry faster. In their haste, one of the men tripped, bumping into a table sending leaves drifting to the ground.

The guard smacked the unfortunate man in the side of his head with the butt of the gun. The man dropped, blood covering the side of his head. The guard barked something, and the men grabbed the fallen man by his arms and hurried on toward the end of the structure, where whitish blocks, of what Skye guessed were drugs, were stacked. There had to be easily two hundred blocks, maybe three.

The men stopped at what looked like a long trough made out of a hollowed out log. Skye looked past it to another open area beyond the building. Leaves lay drying in the sun. That wasn't what caught and held her attention, but what she first took to be a scarecrow.

She gasped. Staked in the middle of the field, with his arms stretch wide, was a decaying corpse. His shirt hung shredded over sunken brown skin turned leather under the sun. Black hair was clumped, matted with debris. The mouth and eyes were wide as if frozen in horror – or agony. As she stared, a bug crawled across the weathered cheek and into the mouth.

Skye gagged and turned, pulling back into her body as her stomach clenched and bile rose. She barely held it down. At the sight of the smugness of the man standing over her, she wished she'd have lost it all over his shoes.

"Tell me seer, what did you see?"

Skye shuddered, locking her arms over her. Turning her face away to block out Vibora's image as she wished she could do with the memory of the dead man.

೦৪৪০

Zac wanted to plow his fist into the man leaning over Skye. Viper fit him well. He was a snake – cold-blooded, slithering, and deadly. Whatever Skye had seen had left her pale and shaken.

More than anything he wanted to go to her, wrap his arms around her and shelter her from the world. All he could do was rest back against the truck and maintain the illusion of a weak, beaten man, he portrayed. He had to be patient and wait for his opportunity. Never had that been so hard, but there were too many men armed and ready to kill for him to act prematurely.

He wasn't surprised to see the old C-130 cargo plane.

They were a favorite with the legal and the unscrupulous for moving cargo. A sturdy machine with a lot of room for cargo, and didn't require a runway, as long as the area was long and smooth enough. He should've figured they'd have something like that.

He had to get to Skye. If possible, keep them from getting her on the plane. If he couldn't stop it, he had to make sure he was on it too.

Having the head man here personally made it all so much more difficult. It spoke of exactly how much he, Vibora, wanted Skye. Still it surprised him the drug lord would risk coming into the United States. Unfortunately, that meant more guards and a better caliber of them.

First thing, he needed to get his hands free. Zac studied the men around him. Coons wasn't as much a threat any longer. Between his injury and his reflexes obviously hampered by painkillers, only his volatile nature made him hard to predict.

Sterling was utterly predictable. He stepped on the back of others, the type who preferred others to do his dirty work and him to step in and finish it off, always looking for the easy route. Zac disliked men like him.

Vibora and his guards were what was worrisome. There was no doubt they'd kill quickly and without much provocation. Vibora would relish in the kill, drawing it out if it served his propose or just for pleasure.

Skye flinched, tightening her arms around herself. "A−," her voice cracked and broke. She swallowed with effort and started again. "I was in a jungle someplace. An area had been cleared but was covered by a camouflage netting." She swallowed again, pulling herself back together with a shaky breath. "There was a crude building. Do you want me to draw it?"

Vibora made a motion and one of the guards walked up the ramp and came back with a pad and pencil that must have been left waiting for just that propose. The guard glared at her as he dropped the items into her lap, pulling back quickly.

Zac realized there was a hint of fear in his reaction. Skye, or at least her ability, made him nervous.

Skye's fingers shook as she sketched. "The building had no sides, just open with long, crude tables. The ones on the end had plants piled on them. The ones on this end," she made quick movements of sketching, "held bricks that I imagine were drugs." She tilted her head up and glared at Vibora challenging him to either deny or confirm. A bit of the spunk Zac associated with her showed.

"At this end, there was a large truck and a small compact-sized one that was an oxidized red. There was a man," she glanced at the guard closest to her. "Dressed like him, but sweatier. He had a gun. He was directing four other men. They showed signs of hard labor, poor conditions and abuse."

Zac wished he could caution her to curb her actions. She might be valuable, but Vibora wouldn't hesitate to hurt her. As if to prove his thought, Vibora lowered his hand to rest on the knife hilt and leaned over her.

Zac prepared himself if he had to react, calculating his moves.

"That is not much information." The drug lord's voice dropped low like steel, his accent ringing heavier. "I expected more from you. The information in the files, if it can be believed, was very detailed."

"Then don't leave dead men staked out for me to find." Skye shot back, not even flinching at his threat. "Did you kill him just for me to see, or did you have another point to make with that poor man?"

Zac lowered his head to hide his reaction. No wonder she looked so pale. He raised his eyes just enough to see Vibora.

The man's lips curled up in a chilling smile. "Two purposes. The workers were protesting, the man tried to negotiate for better conditions. Seems they were unsatisfied with what they were given. They needed a reminder." He placed his hands on the arms of the chair to lean closer, placing his face directly in front of hers. "As do you. The next person you see tied to a stake may be your 'key'."

Skye's hands trembled. She didn't say anything.

Vibora straightened. "We've been on the ground too long. Get them loaded." He walked up the ramp without looking back.

Zac thought about making his move now, but with his hands still fastened behind his back, and the other men armed and on alert, he knew it would be foolhardy.

Before he even had a chance to react, the guard who'd showed hesitancy around Skye grabbed her by the arm and yanked her from the chair. Fortunately, another guard stepped forward catching her other arm, keeping her from falling. They half dragged and half carried her up the ramp.

The plane's engines came to life.

"Move." The guttural word was hard to understand, but the intent was clear as the man beside him jabbed him in the ribs with his gun.

Zac had the guard by almost a foot in height and figured he could take him even with his hands tied, but since he wanted to get to Skye, he didn't protest but staggered to his feet. Sterling moved in front of them with Coons bringing up the rear.

They were halfway to the plane when another roar filled the air and a trio of black vehicles burst out onto the field speeding toward them. The guard on the ramp opened fire, along with the one by Zac. Shots peppered the ground around the plane, several hitting close.

Sterling took off for the plane like a frightened rabbit, hunched over, his hand covering his head. Coons bolted forward. Zac slammed into him, impacting right on his injured shoulder.

The sergeant cried out and went down.

Zac continued his forward motion, ducking his head and ramming into the guard as he started to turn on him. The man staggered. Zac planted his feet and kicked out, his foot catching the guard squarely in the chest. Air escaped him in a violent puff. Zac didn't wait to watch him fall but took off for the plane that was already beginning to move, the ramp starting to rise.

A bullet hit the ground barely missing Zac, spurring him for more speed. He reached the ramp and threw himself on. The guard firing off the end shifted his attention toward him but it was too late.

Zac scissor-kicked catching the guard mid-calf, taking his legs out from under him. The man crashed down. Zac was ready with another kick that caught him in the head and shoulder with enough force that the man dropped off the back as the plane picked up speed.

Zac rolled to his feet staggering into the belly of the plane as the last couple bullets pinged off before the ramp closed all the way. A loud roar reverberated off the walls. The plane jerked and swayed. Zac went with the motion letting it pitch him against the side. He spread his legs wide for balance as the bumping increased.

He took in several deep breaths surveying his surroundings. He was hidden from view for the moment behind a shiny black SUV with dark tinted windows and a stack of crates fastened down under a cargo net. It made great coverage for him but it also didn't allow him to see anything.

He figured he wouldn't have much time when they got into the air before someone came to check on the other guards. About five feet away, he spied the tool locker. It only took a few seconds by feel to open it. Twisting, he studied the contents a second until he had the location firmly in his mind where a pair of heavy duty needle-nose pliers were. Getting hold of them was easy as was turning them. Ramming them between his skin and the plastic tie was the tricky part.

He ignored the pain of the plastic digging into his wrists as he went to work on cutting through the bonds. From the angle he was working, it was hard to apply enough pressure to pull the handles together, still each attempt he made gummed and weakened it until the plastic finally snapped at the same time the ground dropped away and they were airborne.

His muscles ached as he brought his arms forward and shook them to restore circulation. He wiped blood from his wrist onto his pants as he looked for a weapon. Seeing nothing, he turned back to the toolbox grabbing out an awl and several screwdrivers.

He crouched as he made his way along the SUV. Waiting and listening before he dodged to the cargo crate. With his back pressed to it, he eased forward to peer around. The way was clear. He couldn't see anyone. Shifting to the other side he repeated the process.

Skye sat in one of a handful of airline seats that had been bolted to the floor right behind the bulkhead. Sterling was one seat over from her. One of the guards stood over them, another guard was rummaging through a storage compartment just in front of them. Zac pulled back.

He had to hurry and get to Skye so he could get them off the plane before they were out over the ocean. Crouching, and pressed against the pallet, he edged forward. He didn't have to worry about making noise. Not much would be heard over the noise of the plane. The parachutes were conveniently just in front of him, not ten feet from Skye, but he'd have to neutralize the men in the cargo bay before he could go for the chutes.

He peeked out. Both men were now at the storage cabinet, intent on reloading their ammo magazines. Sterling had on a pair of noise canceling headphones. Skye looked sullen in her seat. Her arms wrapped around her as if trying to hold herself together though she looked shattered already.

"I'm coming sweetheart." He sent out the thought, though he knew her ability didn't work that way to let her hear him. He put the screwdrivers in his left hand, keeping the awl in his right. He took a deep breath and stepped clear, throwing the awl. It struck his intended target, sinking deep into the man's chest. The man yelled and fell back against the bulkhead and sagged to the ground.

The other guard spun bringing up his gun. Zac palmed the screwdrivers one after another into his right hand, letting them fly in smooth succession. His aim was true but the poorly weighted instruments weren't as effective as a knife. Two hit handle first, the other struck just as the guard moved, sinking into his arm instead of his chest. Still, they gave him time to rush the guard before he could get his gun up.

Zac led with his fist, catching the guard as the man tried to pull back. The guard's gun strafed the ceiling with bullets before Zac sent the heel of his hand into the man's throat. A scream sounded behind him over the din. He spun as the guard dropped in a heap.

Skye clung and clawed at Sterling as the colonel tried to level a gun at him. Three rounds exploded from the gun, impacting into the cabin door. There was a rushing sound and the plane shuddered. Sterling whipped the gun around to strike Skye.

Zac caught his arm and rammed his fist into Sterling's face, crushing bone. He didn't have time to do more as the door to the cockpit opened. He threw himself to the side barely before the bullet meant for him plowed into Sterling. Zac drove himself into the door, smashing it back into the shooter. He grabbed the arm forcing it up, trying for the gun.

Shots rang out. The man he struggled with jerked and lost hold of the gun, which clattered to the floor. The man toppled forward on to Zac, taking him to the ground along with him.

Vibora stepped through the door. "More than a key." The drug lord drew his knife.

Zac rolled free and to his feet, dodging the swipe of the blade that if connected, would have sliced open his stomach. Vibora swung back, the knife nicking Zac's shoulder before he could thrust his arm up knocking the blade away. Zac drove his fist into Vibora then blocked a blow.

The plane jolted staggering the men, allowing Vibora to break free. Venom burned in the man as he eyed him. The knife whipped out between them showing obvious skill as the drug lord tested and challenged him.

Zac waited. He was ready for Vibora's attack. When it came, it was in a blur of movement. Vibora struck, slashing out. Zac stepped in, catching his wrist, forcing his hands up. Vibora kicked out.

Zac side stepped, twisting away, never releasing Vibora's hand. Out of the corner of his eye, Zac saw the guard he'd stuck with the awl pull himself up, raising the gun he'd been holding.

Vibora took his moment of distraction as an opportunity to attack. He rammed his elbow into Zac's temple.

Zac staggered, losing grip with one hand. He hit Vibora in the chin snapping his head back and twisted, driving him into the guard, knocking the guard back against the bulkhead.

Vibora forced the knife down toward Zac's face, the tip nearly impaling his cheek. Zac tightened his hold, locking his muscles, forcing Vibora back. He freed one hand to grip the front of his shirt and lifted the man in the air and heaved him away. The man flew four feet before smashing into the bay side and dropping to the floor.

Vibora remained still. Zac sucked in a breath and stepped over to him, pushing him over with his foot, ready for another attack. None came. The wicked knife was buried deep in the snake's side. Venom still showed in his eyes but it was fading.

Vibora's gaze went to Skye. He tried to speak but blood gurgled up instead of words. He fell back. The Viper was dead.

Zac turned as a bullet ricocheted off the wall not an inch from his head. He dropped and twisted. The guard slumped back against the bulkhead as a burst of pops thundered through the bay. Zac flinched but felt no impacts. A dark stain spread over the man's chest as his head tilted to the side.

Zac's gaze shifted to Skye sitting on the floor by the seats, the other guard's gun locked in her hands, extended out in front of her body. "Skye." He reached her, wrapping his hand over hers as the gun slipped from her fingers.

More than anything, he wanted to pull her to him and comfort her but was aware of the continued danger from anyone remaining on the plane.

"Stay down and wait for me." He gave her fingers a quick squeeze before going to the wall and grabbing a coil of webbing.

"What are we going to do?" Skye said loud enough to be heard over the noise in the bay.

He hooked one end in the tie-down ring on the wall then stretched it in front of the door, wrapping the webbing around the handle several times. "Get out of here, but first I want to make sure no one else tries to kill us before we leave." He hooked in to another ring and started to ratchet it down tight, until satisfied there was no way the door was going to open.

He went to where the parachutes hung on the wall, surprised to find one designed for tandem jumps. He took it down, checked all the straps then put it on. Grabbing a couple pairs of goggles, he return to Skye. She had climbed up in the seat and waited. No fear shown in her face as she looked at him.

"I found this in Sterling's pocket." She held out a cell-phone.

"That'll come in handy when we land." He took it and slipped it into his pocket. "Time to go. Do you trust me?"

"Yes. I've jumped with you a number of times."

He couldn't help smile, knowing what she meant. She had been with him often. He'd known when she was there. "This is going to be a little different, but don't worry, I'm very good at this."

"I know." Again there was no hesitation in her.

"You're going to be strapped to me." He held out the harness to her, talking as he strapped her in. "You don't have to do anything but try not to smack me in the nose. I'll do everything. I'll open the chute as soon as it's safe to keep our speed down, and it will be less jarring." He tightened the last buckle, then framed her face in his hands and kissed her. They broke off at the sound of pounding at the door.

"Our cue." He helped her to the control panel for the ramp, then hooked her to him and activated the control. Air whooshed in so loud it made it impossible to be heard. He stopped the ramp when it extended out level, then pulling the final screwdriver from the toolbox rammed it into the mechanism disabling it.

Skye wrapped her arms around herself as he locked an arm around her waist, lifted her and walked off the end of the ramp.

ᚲ৪ᛒᚲ

Skye gasped when they dropped into open air, then clamped her mouth shut. They rolled once, and she found herself looking straight down. The setting sun lit everything with a fiery glow. It was spectacular. Butterflies zinged around her stomach. Zac was right, different from before but knowing he was with her made it not scary.

She felt the jerk as the chute deployed and looked up to

see the white, green, and orange material fill with air. A shout of exhilaration exploded from her. Behind her, she felt him laugh.

"You like it?" he called in her ear.

"Yes. This is amazing. Something I always wanted to try." She craned her head around in an effort to see him. She couldn't get a good look but the brush of his lips on her cheek was enough.

"There's a town to our right. I'm going to angle us over there. The air current is already carrying us that way.

She saw where he was talking about and felt the subtle shift in that direction. As they drifted, all the danger they had faced the last couple days seemed to float free.

The lower they dropped, the more distinguishable everything became. Patches of color and faint lines became individual fields, trees and roads. With expert work Zac brought them down over an open field next to a road.

"I want you to tuck your legs up," Zac said. "Let me take the landing."

"But–,"

"I don't want your ankle injured anymore. Wrap your hands around my arms just before we touch down."

"Okay." Skye held her breath, watching the ground come closer. Six feet from the ground she reached up, wrapped her hands around his biceps and pulled up her legs. Zac's feet hit the ground. He stumbled, but kept his footing as the chute billowed behind them.

"We made it." Skye let out a little squeal.

"Did you doubt it?" He released her harness, lowered her down and turned her in his arms.

"No." She wrapped her arms around his neck. "It's just hard to believe. It's over."

He kissed her hard before breaking the contact. "Not quite." Zac pulled Sterling's phone from his pocket and he made a call.

Skye lowered her head to his chest, letting go of the

fear she hadn't been able to shed yet. It seemed so unreal that they could actually be safe, that Coons, Sterling and Vibora could be gone. Were they? Vibora certainly was, and she was certain Sterling was. But Coons, what happened to him? And where had Botts gone? She pressed tighter into Zac, listening to the beat of his heart. He was safe.

She opened her eyes and her gaze fell on his arm. Blood darkened the material.

"You're hurt."

He glanced at the cut on his arm and looked away, continuing his conversation.

With nothing to clean it, Skye pulled up the material enough to get a good look. It was about two inches long and deep enough she figured it need stitches. Still, it didn't appear to be too bad. She kept the panic that threatened her down.

He was safe. It was over.

Zac continued talking for quite a while before disconnecting. "Someone will collect us. Let's get to the road. You know, I could really go for one of the candy bars from your pack."

"I want a large, medium rare steak and steak fries."

"Oh, the perfect woman."

"Do you think we'll ever get our stuff back?"

"The agents that raided the field will have recovered it. So I'd say there's a good chance." He kissed her again then lifted her in his arms, carrying her to the road. They were only settled on the ground to wait for a couple minutes before flashing lights appeared in the distance, speeding their way.

Zac stood and waved. The highway patrol vehicle stopped beside him.

"Colonel Masters?" the officer asked stepping out.

"Yes."

"I've been asked to transport you. I've also been asked

for you not to discuss details between yourselves during the trip."

"I understand. We could go for some food, if possible." Zac helped Skye up. "She also needs someone to check her ankle."

"Well, if that can wait, it would be better, but I don't see why we can't get you something to eat on the way."

They stopped in town long enough for them to wash up and get something at the fast-food place. They savored each bite of the burger and fries.

"Not quite a steak," Zac commented.

"But it works." Skye sighed then curled into his side and went right to sleep.

Skye woke to be hustled into a building and separated from Zac. Questioning started. She hardly got through it the first time when a general showed up, plus agents from three different agencies.

With clearance from the general, she went into more detail of what was in the reports she suspected Sterling and Coons of selling. She was assured that warrants would be issued for Dr. Botts and Wesley Wringer to be brought in to find the depth of their involvement.

The general finally stood. "I want to thank you. I'm sorry for what you went through, but all in all, it sounds like it was a good thing. From what I've been told, the drug lord you brought down was an extremely," he paused, "nasty individual."

"That's right." The man from DEA came up beside the general. "We been trying to get him for some time. The only good thing about him, is he has taken out quite a few of his competitors that were equally as ... as nasty." The man smiled adding emphasis on the end.

"You were able to get him?" Skye asked.

The smile that man gave her brightened. "We were able to persuade the pilot of the plane to land. It was quite easy with his tail open and he wasn't going to make to his destination." We found Colonel Sterling, Vibora and two of his men dead in the cargo bay. Another was still alive, as were the men in the cockpit. There was also twenty million dollars in cash on the plane."

"What?" Skye gasped.

"That's right. It looks like you and Lt. Colonel Masters are up for quite a reward."

"Where is Lt. Colonel Masters?" She stumbled on his name.

"Waiting right outside the door. He's been waiting for you to be finished to go to the hospital with you." The agent went to the door and opened it.

Skye lost what he was saying the moment Zac stepped through the door. She held out her arms as he crossed to her. Heedless of all the people in the room, he wrapped his arms around her and pulled her to him and kissed her.

Skye felt herself drifting, but when she opened her eyes to look in his, everything was right in the world. She was where she was supposed to be.

"It's finally over, now." She breathed deep and smiled.

"Well," Zac drew out the word. "Not quite. We still have to get married, but I think I've pulled enough strings to get that set up for later on today, if you're up to it."

"Today?"

"Someone needs to watch out for you. You need a fulltime guard and I have the qualifications for the post."

"Post?"

"Yes, you see I'm needing a new one since I retired."

"So you're going to take over watching me."

"As I said, someone's got to do it."

She heard the teasing lilt in the words. "It took a full installation to do it before." She purred the words.

"Yeah, but I'll be able to do it from a lot closer." He dipped his head, his lips brushed hers, and his voice grew husky. "That's why marriage."

"What about that I love you?"

"That just makes it convenient because I love you too."
He kissed her again, deeper, with the promise of all the things she'd never been able to see before in her future.

Epilogue

Twinges of nerves fluttered through Skye's stomach as they crossed the bridge over the small creek and followed the road winding through the trees. She knew the house was just up ahead. She'd scouted out the whole area in her mind, unable to help but peek.

This was her new home – her new family. The closest people to Zac. Skye hope they'd like her and not be freaked out by what she could do. Not that she'd be doing it often now, but she had agreed when the General asked her that if ever needed, she would help.

Zac reached over the console and gave her hand a squeeze. "You okay? You seem a little nervous."

"I am." Over the last two and a half weeks she'd grown used to holding hands. Zac was always there to support her, but it was more, he seemed to like to be in contact with her. From the moment they said their "I dos", they'd become one. Giddy pleasure raced through her at the thought.

It had been a very simple wedding, just the judge that agreed to do the ceremony, and the men in his squad, who had driven over to be with them. They held the ceremony in a little wooded glade, with a stream running through, similar to the one they'd found refuge in when running for their lives.

There had been some teasing at how fast the mighty had fallen, but there had also been acceptance. Maybe because they trusted Zac, or because she'd known them right off though just actually meeting them for the first time. She'd been surrounded by the strong men, and enveloped into the unit, just how she had been later that night in Zac's arms.

After retrieving her suitcases and his truck, which had a new set of tires thanks to Sterling, and making arrangements for everything else she owned to be packed and shipped, they spent two weeks on the road for a honeymoon. And now they were here.

Through the trees the way opened to a stucco, rock and wood beam house. The door opened before they reached it and a thin, medium-height woman with brown-blonde hair flew out the door followed by a carbon copy of Zac except his hair was a touch longer. They came down the steps as Zac helped her out of the truck. Steadying her until her crutches were in place, he turned to receive a hug from his brother.

Skye smiled at Marley who beamed back.

"It really is something seeing the two men together." Marley wiped moisture off her cheek. "Hormones. Welcome."

Skye felt the same moisture gather in her eyes but didn't know what her excuse was. They'd only been married two weeks. She didn't think she could be pregnant, though Zac had told her Marley was after just a couple weeks. No, her tears had to be for the pull on her heart for the two men and to having a new family.

The next instant the brothers opened their arms and pulled her and Marley into the hug. Skye didn't need to use her gift of seeing or any other to know what the future would bring as love filled the circle of her family.

About the Author

I grew up in a small town in Wyoming loving the outdoors, sports, art, and reading Hardy Boys books. After reading them all at least a half dozen times, I started writing my own stories.

For thirty-three years I was married to a wonderful, honorable man. I'm mother of five children and grandmother of nine, eight boys and one girl, with hopefully more to come. I love traveling. Through my husband's work and vacations, I have visited much of the United States, all over Europe, Canada, Mexico, China, Thailand, Cambodia and Australia, giving me many intriguing locations and experiences for my stories.

I am a storyteller. I write the classic hero story because I think there's a need for more heroes, love, and adventure in our lives. I'm not out to change the world with my writing; I'm just hoping to make your day a little better.

Hope you enjoy.
Alysia S. Knight

Please feel free to visit me through my website:

www.alysiasknight.com